Desired By The Single Dad

The Single Dads Club

Sierra Shipley

Table of Contents

Books By Sierra

The Claiming Her Series
His Temptation
His Disaster
His Reward
His Challenge

The Rose Prairie Series
All books in The Rose Prairie Series are standalone set in the small town of Rose Prairie.
All Tangled Up
Tied In Nots
It Had To Be You

Interconnected Stand-Alone
Yes, Captain
Hey, Neighbor

The Single Dads Club
Loved by the Single Dad
Nanny for the Single Dad
Desired by the Single Dad

Prologue

Sutton
Two Months Ago

"D on't look, but a seriously hot guy is checking you out at the bar." Kelly lifts her mojito to her mouth, taking a large gulp.

Shock and flattery have my eyes bulging. The urge to scan the dimly lit bar is overwhelming. Out of the dozens of times we've come to this bar, not once have I caught someone's eye.

"You can't say that and then not tell me to look." Maybe this is the universe sending me a graduation present. The vodka cranberry warms my belly. Liquid courage steels my veins and I sneak a look around the bar.

She rolls her eyes, a smile tugging at her lips. "Corner. Three o'clock."

"Corner? Oh god, is it a creep?" It would be just my to catch the eye of the resident creeper.

"No," she snorts. "I told you he was hot." She glances back at the corner. "I mean, if you don't want him, I do."

"Ugh. Fine." I take one more sip for reinforcement before sneaking a peek. "Ho-ly shit."

"I know. I bet it's your ass that lured him in. I'd kill to have your ass, especially in that dress."

Kelly's comment slips right past me as I make eye contact with the man. He's definitely looking at me. There's no mistaking the hunger in his gaze. Instead of being intimidated, I'm honestly turned on.

He's tall and put together, not like the guys in my graduating class. He seems to ooze confidence, which I find irresistible.

"What do I do?"

Kelly's laughter isn't encouraging. "He's coming over here, so you better figure it out fast. Just bounce your tits in his face or something. Use those curves to your advantage."

I love her—my forever hype woman. During our four years at Liberty College, her constant encouragement helped grow my confidence in my curves. The "freshman fifteen" was something I'd heard of, but I wasn't prepared for more than that. It looks like I've inherited the curves from the women on my dad's side of the family, all soft bellies and round hips.

I prepare myself the only way I know how—gulping down what's left of my drink.

"Can I get you another one?"

The sound of his voice has me sucking in a breath that I immediately regret. My drink slips down my windpipe and I sputter, my eyes watering as I fight the urge to cough. Kelly laughs, covering her mouth with her drinks before slipping away into the crowd.

I hold up a finger to my new companion, asking for a minute as I try not to choke. He smiles warmly at me while I compose myself.

Up close, he's even more handsome. Older than me, but still charming with his crinkling green eyes and tempting smile.

"I could use a drink." I smile back at him and offer my hand, leaning closer to be heard over the music. "I'm Sutton." Rough, manly hands engulf mine, and I imagine what they would feel like on my body. His cologne washes over me, hitting me like a cloud. I breathe him in, my hum of appreciation drowned out by the loud bar.

"Wells. It's nice to meet you, Sutton." Hot breath whispers through my hair, making me shiver. "What are you drinking?"

4

I hold up my second empty glass this evening, repeating my go-to order of vodka cranberry. Two drinks is normally when I cut myself off, but I'm in unprecedented territory.

I'll pay for my sins tomorrow, but tonight, I say to hell with it.

KEYS CLATTER TO THE floor the moment the door closes behind us. I've been flirting with danger in the form of a man and I'm not holding back any longer.

One drink turned into two, and my inhibitions waltzed out the door with a pep in her step. By the time Wells asked if I wanted to get out of there, I was practically in his lap, the two of us unable to keep our hands off each other.

The drive to this house was a practice in restraint. One that snapped the second we got inside.

I rip through the buttons of his shirt, frantic to feel his skin beneath it. Wells pulls down the neckline of my dress, revealing my tanned round breast.

"Are you okay with this?" he asks between fevered kisses along my skin.

I drag his mouth to mine, moaning against his lips. "More than okay."

Wells moans as I stroke his hard cock through his jeans. My pussy clenches in response. I've never been so turned on by a sound in my life.

He slides his hands up my thighs, pushing my tight dress up to my hips. A hunger in his eyes wipes away any uncertainty I feel about my body.

Fresh embarrassment settles through me when I remember what pair of underwear I put on. I didn't care because there was zero chance of going home with someone, but now that I'm here? I just had to throw on the tried-and-true, reliable tummy control panties that rise to my waist.

Oh my god, I'm having my very own Bridget Jones moment. Only worse because it's happening to *me*.

Wells doesn't seem to care. All concern regarding my undergarments disappears the moment he cups me through the silky fabric. I gasp against his mouth as feverish need blazes like lightning straight to my core.

Now I'm even more desperate to have his hands all over me. To have my hands all over him.

Wells must sense my desperation because we become a flurry of scattered clothes. Wells leads me down the hallway, ricocheting off walls as we devour each other.

I've never had such a fierce sexual draw to someone, and maybe it's the alcohol, but I've never felt this before. This desperation. An overwhelming need.

I'm so lost in him it doesn't even register that we're in a bedroom until we're on the bed. Wells pulls me on top of him, his hands gripping my hips and rocking me against his hard length.

"God, you look so good, Sutton." I look down on him, on his body tensing underneath me with pleasure and shudder as his cock presses against my clit. "Nightstand," he rumbles. "Top drawer."

I rock against him once more before doing as I'm told, fishing out a condom from the box in the back of the drawer. He takes it from me and I watch with eager eyes as he unrolls the condom down his impressive length. When his eyes flick up to mine, it's the burning heat lingering in his gaze that has me positioning myself over him and sinking down.

My eyes roll with each inch, my breath hitching from the blissful feeling of fullness. Wells groans and my muscles clench around him, making him hiss and grind me down on his pelvis. "If you keep doing that, I'm not gonna last long, and I plan on taking my time."

"Really?" I ask, swiveling my hips, loving the feeling of him deep inside me. "How long are we talking?"

Wells sits up and latches his mouth around my nipple. On instinct, I hold him closer to my chest, his hair sliding through my fingers. "All night if you think you can keep up?"

A desperate moan escapes my lips. I can't take it anymore. He's been driving me wild all night and I'm ready to ride his cock with wild abandon. A night like this only happens once and I'm going to drown in the blissful sin.

I move, bouncing on his cock as he clutches me to his chest. We set a quick rhythm with him fucking me from beneath as I sink down, hitting a spot that has me dragging my nails down his shoulders.

Lost in the feel of him, his breath tickling my skin, his hot mouth sucking my nipple, is something I've never experienced. All I know is him. The intoxicating smell of his skin, rough hands on my hips, his cock hitting me just where I need him. It doesn't take long before I'm whimpering with need. "I'm close. I'm about to—"

"That's it," Wells praises, his hand slipping between us. His thumb brushes against my clit, adding the perfect amount of pressure and with one last thrust, I explode, focused on nothing other than the roar of pleasure overloading my senses. "Fuck, you feel amazing."

While I'm still reeling from my orgasm, Wells flips us, pounding into my still pulsing pussy. My thighs lock around his hips and I writhe against him, new heat blooming in my core.

I can't stop myself from moaning with each intense thrust. Sweat coats my skin. My body is burning for him.

Wells moans and I slide my eyes open, meeting his unexpecting gaze. Something wild grows between our stares. An unexpected climax shatters through me, sending Wells over the edge with a groan.

Hours later, I sneak out his bedroom door. Wells sleeps peacefully, his strong back rising with each breath. Something about this moment, the way the moonlight streaks across the bed, how his arm drapes across the mattress where I laid, has me pausing. I don't want him to become a blurred image from one wild night. I want to picture him as he is now when I think back on this night and remember how he made me feel.

On shaky legs, I slip through the door, gathering my scattered clothing and dress hastily in the dark. I text Kelly a pin of my location and never look back. Even though every part of me wants to crawl back into his bed and never leave.

Chapter One

Sutton

Present Day

The car idles on the curb in a modest neighborhood in front of a small house. My stomach twists in knots and I cover my mouth, fighting back the bile that seems to be never ending.

"Did you puke? Are you puking?" Kelly dry heaves through the phone, coughing and complaining. "Oh my god, if you throw up, then I'm throwing up and I'm not even there." She's been a rock with this whole situation, but she cannot handle vomit. Ironic, considering she's a nurse.

I gag involuntarily and pray like hell I don't throw up. Saliva pools in my mouth and I swallow convulsively, breathing deeply. Eyes sealed shut as a last defense, I flip the AC to the highest setting.

"Sorry," she says, "I'm being dramatic. Are you okay?"

The bout of nausea dissipates slowly, and I sigh with relief. "I'm good." I lean my head against the headrest, letting the cool air calm me. "Are you sure this is the right place?"

"Positive. That's the exact location you sent me to come to pick you up looking like you'd been fucked by a god. What was his name again?"

This is what has my stomach more messed up than normal. Well, more than my new normal. "Wells," I breathe.

"That's right. Are you going to woman up and go tell him or what?" A phone rings in the background and she curses. "I've got to go, but you've got this, Sutton. No matter what, you've got me."

I manage a quick thanks before the line clicks. She's right though. I need to step up and get this done. It's the right thing to do.

Knowing it's the right thing to do doesn't make it any easier.

I run through my plan, plotting out exactly how I'm going to explain this. For all I know, he never wanted to see me again, and now I'm going to stand on his doorstep and deliver some shocking news.

Before I can talk myself into putting the car in drive and hightailing it out of here, I kill the engine and push from the car.

My heart pounds with each step up the driveway. The August sun heats the top of my head and warms my tan skin. I suck in a steadying breath as I step up on the porch and ring the doorbell.

Anxiety rips through me. There's no telling what he's going to say, but I can try to control the situation. At least, I think I can. I stare at my linked fingers, focusing on keeping my breathing even when the door squeaks open.

"Hi." A tiny voice startles me. All plans drift from my mind as I look at the small kid behind the storm door. He can't be more than kindergarten age, if that. Shiny blonde hair and large green eyes peer at me.

"Um—" I'm speechless. Wells can't have a kid, right? I replay the memories of messy clothes and hastened touches, but I remember nothing about a kid.

The boy tilts his head, his large green eyes blinking up at me. "Who are you?"

"I think I need to go..." I turn to step off the porch when a familiar voice comes from inside the house, making me pause.

"Tristan, what have I told you about opening the door?"

His voice has the same effect on me as it did the first time. Goosebumps prickle my skin, despite the warm air and my growing anxiety.

Oh god, does he have a wife? A family?

I'm a home-wrecker. The other woman coming in to ruin the perfect family.

He wasn't wearing a ring; I remind myself. So what if he already has a kid? It just means he's prepared.

Unless... he doesn't want another kid.

I'm gonna throw up.

His silhouette emerges from the dark shadows of the house. He's exactly as I remember him. His brown hair isn't as messy, but his strong brows, kind eyes, and firm jaw are just as I remember. I don't stop myself from dragging my gaze over his broad shoulders, his t-shirt clinging in all the right places to the muscles I know lie underneath.

The boy turns toward him with a look on his face that I would normally find funny. "I was here first," he says like it justifies everything.

Wells doesn't seem to notice. His wide eyes are glued to me through the glass door. "Sutton?" his stunned voice is more of a gasp.

Trying to compose myself, I give him a tight smile and an awkward wave. "Hi."

Wells pushes past the little boy and steps out onto the porch. He's so much taller than I remember.

"I, um..." My eyes widen in panic, glancing back at the boy behind the door. All my careful planning has flown out the window.

"Tristan, go play inside." Wells never once looks away from me. It's like he's seeing me for the first time and I'll disappear if he turns around.

Tristan's eyes light up. "Video games?"

"Sure." With a happy little laugh, Tristan takes off running, a sound of triumph trailing behind him. If I wasn't distracted by my rushing thoughts and the impressive man standing in front of me, I might've laughed.

I suck in a steadying breath, knowing the words I say next will flip his world upside down. "Sorry to just drop by unannounced, but I didn't have many options."

Wells steps onto the porch, letting the door click closed behind him. "I thought I'd never see you again. You left before I could get your number."

I wince. "Yeah, I don't make a habit of going home with men, and I guess I panicked." We stand in awkward silence for a moment before regaining my courage. "I, um, well, there's no other way to say this...I'm pregnant," I rush, "and it's yours. I mean, there isn't anyone else. So..."

All color drains from his face. I completely understand the shock of the situation. Hell, I had a mental breakdown when the word "pregnant" popped up on the little digital screen. But I've had a couple of weeks to adjust to the news that I'm going to be a mom.

"You're. Pregnant." He says the words like he's never heard them uttered before.

"I understand that this is a lot to take in." Wells' back hits the house with a thunk. "You're under no obligations—"

"Hold on," he says, cutting me off with an outstretched hand.

"Right." He needs time to adjust. I might have a planned out speech, but he's hearing everything for the first time.

Wells' chest heaves with every inhale. A large palm rests against his chest as if his heart is about to burst through it. If I didn't know any better, I'd say he's close to having a panic attack.

I clasp my hands in front of me, not knowing what to do. I want to reach out, rub his shoulders in comfort, but we're practically strangers. Yeah, he knows the shape of my body, the feel of my skin, but in the stark daylight, everything's different. So instead, I stand awkwardly in front of him, biting my lip, and wait.

"How far along?" he rasps, eyes pinned to the concrete porch, and he swallows hard.

My throat feels thick and I clear it. "I think about eight weeks. I'll know for sure at my doctor's appointment in a little over a week."

He nods in a daze.

"I'm keeping it," I sputter. "I need you to know that. It might not be ideal, but it's my baby, and I'm going to take care of it. You don't have to do anything you don't want to. If that means I do this alone, then I will." Determination leaks from my voice.

Somewhere during my speech, Wells' gaze switched to my face. His sun tanned skin is still a pale green, but he stands upright. "Not alone," he states. "You're not alone in this, Sutton. I want you to know that." He reaches for my clasped hands, squeezing them lightly. "We're in this together."

Chapter Two

Wells

Blood drains from my face, my heart pounds out of my chest. Sutton walked away five minutes ago and still I can't get myself under control.

Tristan sits in front of the television playing Mario Cart, completely oblivious to the fact that his father is freaking the fuck out.

Air refuses to fill my lungs. Not again. I can't have it happen again.

Closing my eyes, I focus on my son's excited shouts. Darkness descends on me. Inhale, hold, exhale.

It's fine.

She's fine.

I'm fine.

That all too familiar panic settles, only enough to mask the raging storm within me.

I'm having a baby. *We're* having a baby. She's carrying my child and there's no way I'm letting her do it alone. I *can't* let her do it alone. Not with what I know it can cost.

"Dad, you wanna play?" Tristan turns to look at me, his face expectant.

I swallow, forcing a smile. "Not right now, bud. I've, uh, got some things I need to do first."

He shrugs, turning back to the screen. "Okay."

"Don't play for too long. We're going to Cole's house here soon."

"I know," he says, eyes glued to the screen as he starts a new race.

I lock my bedroom door and sit on the edge of the bed. The cool darkness is a balm to my overheated nerves.

That night—the night I met Sutton, the night she got pregnant—runs through my head. Hell, it's been on repeat since she snuck out. Long, loose waves cocooning us as she rides me. Soft, full lips moaning my name. The feel of her cunt squeezing my cock as she comes.

All thought ceased to exist when I saw her in that bar. A neon halo drew my eyes right to her and I couldn't look away. With her skin tight dress and mouth watering curves, I was done for.

It's been years since I'd felt this type of intense attraction. This electricity for another person pulsing beneath my skin, sinking into my marrow until I couldn't fight against it. And god help me, I still can't.

Even as she was telling me my world was changing, I couldn't stop looking at her. Even as the breath left my lungs, as panic flooded through me, I couldn't deny how much I wanted her.

Sutton slipped out of my door and out of my life. I thought I'd never see her again, but she came back. And she's pregnant, carrying my child.

Our child.

Tears sting my eyes, and I blink them back. I never thought I'd have this again. After Sara, the possibility of it all slipped through my fingers. The future we had so carefully planned disappeared before my eyes.

But now it's been reborn.

A whirlpool of emotions drags me under. Everything I've felt, hoped for, dreamed of. Nightmares and realties, joy and pain, hope and utter helplessness. I'm drowning in it all, sitting with the pain and breathing through the nervous excitement of having another child.

Sunlight dims in the window, the day turning from a bright summer afternoon to the low glow of the coming evening.

Tap, tap, tap.

Small fingers rap against the closed door. "Is it almost time to go? I'm hungry."

Oh shit.

"Um, yeah bud. Get your shoes on and I'll be out in a minute." Hair slips through my fingers before dragging down my face.

"Oo-kay." He's running down the hallway in a rush to see his friends.

Time to pull my shit together.

"LOOK WHO SHOWED UP." Cole slaps me on the shoulder before turning back to the tv, flipping through channels before settling on ESPN.

Tristan is already running around the yard with Harrison, Jett, and Marie. It's Sunday night, and we're here, but my mind is somewhere else. "Yeah."

The door to the patio opens with Grant carrying an aluminum covered tray. His girlfriend, Hazel, sticks her head through the door. "Hey, Wells. Haven't seen you in a while." The wind blows her auburn waves into her face.

"Been busy." Busy freaking the fuck out over the fact that I'm about to be a dad. Again. I've made excuses, dodged our Sunday get-togethers to avoid their questions about my night out. I'm not ready to tell them. I don't know if I'll ever be ready.

Not when every fiber of my being buzzes with barely hidden panic.

A blonde woman pushes past Hazel, a child's cup in hand. "Marie, want your juice?" Brown curls bounce as Marie toddles her way across the yard, reaching for the outstretched cup.

"What do you say, Marie?" Cole asks his two-year-old daughter. She mumbles a word that sounds like 'thanks' before darting off to chase after her brother. "Wells, this is Joanna, our nanny."

She smiles politely and waves. "It's nice to meet you, Wells. I'm glad I could finally see the trio in person."

"See, I told you," Hazel says, stepping up to her shoulder. "He's not a ghost."

Grant lights the grill, balling up the aluminum that covered the tray. "Leave the man alone. He's been busy."

"What?" Hazel says innocently. "I've been telling Jo about the single dad's club for forever and Wells has been M.I.A."

"Don't worry, I knew you were real." Joanna says to me with a polite smile.

"Thanks."

Hazel sucks in a deep breath. "Well, we're leaving now." She crosses the patio, kissing Grant lightly. "See you later." My best friend smiles down at his girlfriend, his eyes full of something I haven't felt in a long time.

Cole's son Jett runs over, wrapping his arms around Joanna's legs as he says goodbye. She's been their nanny for a little over a month now, and it's clearly going well. Grant mentioned that he's seen a change in Cole. He's been running himself ragged the last several years trying to keep up with everything, and I'm glad he's found someone that helps him find balance.

After dinner, the boys run in and out of the back door, most likely making a mess and leaving chaos in their wake. Marie sleeps on her father's chest, her cherub cheeks pink from the late August heat.

Will I have a daughter of my own to cherish, or will I have another son? I think I'd like to have a girl. She'll have me wrapped around her finger with a single look, just like her mother.

Sutton.

The completely gorgeous woman who's carrying my child. How does she feel about all this? She's strong, I can tell that much. Much stronger than me.

Fuck, is she freaking out too?

"You feelin' alright?" Grant's concerned gaze trains on me. "You seem...off."

I clear my throat. "Uh, yeah. All good."

Cole raises an eyebrow. "Work going okay?"

I suck in a deep breath, letting it and my thoughts out slowly. "Just bought a few more trucks and hired some new crew."

"I'm glad you got some time to yourself, then." Cole says with a smirk, his hand rubbing down his daughter's back. "Hey, what'd you do that night, anyway?"

"I'm sure he got up to trouble," Grant says with a laugh. "The man looked completely relaxed when he came by to pick up Tristan. Dude was practically high."

I shake my head. Let them think what they want. They don't need to know I spent my night buried deep in the woman who's now carrying my child.

Our night together was electric. Sparks flew the moment her eyes locked on mine across the dim bar. Her curves, mouthwatering in that skin tight dress, were even more tempting out of it. I couldn't control myself with her.

And now I'm out of control. Spiraling every other minute knowing that anything can happen and I've already failed once.

Tristan's blonde hair shines under the lights strung up above us. "Dad, can I have a popsicle?" Red is smeared across his lips and dribbles down his chin.

Cole stifles a laugh while Grant sighs. I lean back, looking through the doors that lead into the kitchen. Harrison peeks from around the counter, a purple popsicle in hand. "Looks like you already had one."

His eyes narrow. "No, I didn't."

Grant pulls out his phone. "Come here, Tristan." My son turns towards him as Grant snaps a picture. "Look at this and then tell us you didn't have one already."

"We don't lie, son." I lean forward, catching my son's downcast gaze. "Tell the truth."

His little chin wobbles. "But I want another one. Jett said we could."

Cole mutters a curse, balancing Marie on one arm as he stands. "You've gotta be kidding me."

"You're going to clean up your mess and then we're going home." My son whines. "Now."

Shoulders slumped, Tristan follows Cole into the kitchen.

Grant looks at the picture he took and laughs. "Why do they think they can lie like that?"

"My question is why did he come ask when he's already had one?" I shake my head, chuckling. "We're bound to get phone calls from jail when they're teenagers. It's a good thing Cole's a lawyer." He's a corporate lawyer, but I'm sure he'll be able to pull some strings.

"Nah. We've got time to teach them some common sense."

Cicadas chirp in the darkness. After several minutes of quiet, I ask, "We just going to ignore the nanny thing?"

Grant laughs. "Do you think she knows how he looks at her?"

"And she's living with them? Cole doesn't stand a chance." I lean back into my seat, tipping the beer bottle up to my lips.

"Hazel seems to think there's more going on."

"You mean Hazel knows there's more going on, but you're not going to tell me?" Grant's girlfriend seems to gather information like a squirrel gathers nuts. Except that she's terrible at hiding them.

He smiles, but says nothing.

The doors slide open. "Looks like they each had about three popsicles based on the wrappers left on the floor." Cole sits on the other end of the patio furniture and sighs. "I'm making them wipe everything down and clean up all the toys." His eyes slide open, his brows rising. "What?"

"Oh, nothing," I say, grinning at Grant.

DESIRED BY THE SINGLE DAD

Grant snorts. "We'll let you know later."

Chapter Three

Wells

I'm early.

    Sweat beads on my forehead despite the cool air of the waiting room. Women of all ages sit quietly, waiting to get called back to an exam room. Infants cry from their car seats as new mothers hurry to shush them.

Memories of a very different time plague my addled mind. I run a hand down my face as if to wash them away.

"Sorry. Sorry I'm late." Sutton comes rushing in, taking the seat next to me. She sets her bag on the floor before brushing hair out of her face. "I left work as soon as I could, and then hit every red light on the way. Have you been here long?"

I shake my head. "No, but I was starting to worry."

She chuckles. "Nothing to worry about. Just running late." Her small hand pats my denim clad knee.

An overwhelming sense of desire flames through me. More recent memories of rushed touches and gentle caresses flood my mind. It's an unexpected visceral reaction, and it leaves me reeling.

She's so beautiful. Her long raven hair hangs over her shoulder in loose, silken curls. The summer dress is both professional and enough to drive me crazy. Everything about her drives me crazy. The sweep of her waist to her hips, the glowing gaze of her brown eyes.

Sutton doesn't seem to notice or have the same reaction as I do. Instead, she simply walks to the reception desk to check in and sits back down beside me. "You okay?" Her eyebrows furrow, and I force myself to relax.

"Yeah," I sigh, leaning back in the chair. "It's been a while since I've been to one of these appointments."

Her lips pull up in a soft smile. "Tristan, right?"

My son's face appears in my mind. He looks so much like his mother. I smile. "Yeah. He's five, about to turn six in December."

"He seems like he's a lot of fun."

"He is."

We fall silent, neither one of us sure what to do. We barely know each other, and here we are trying to make awkward small-talk in a gynecologist waiting room.

There's so much I want to learn about her, but it feels strange to do it here. "Are there any forms you have to fill out?"

Sutton's staring across the room at a young woman rubbing her large pregnant belly. "What?" I repeat the question. "Oh, uh, no. I did it online after I made the appointment. I hope you don't mind that I made you an emergency contact. Just in case."

The "just in case" hangs in the air between us. I know firsthand how devastating those words can be.

I nod. "Thank you. I uh—"

"Sutton Boyd?" An older nurse in pink scrubs calls from the doorway to the exam rooms.

Sutton stands, gathering up her belongings.

I'm not sure what to do. Should I follow her? Wait here? She said I was welcome at her appointments, but does that mean she's okay with me being back there with her?

Sutton takes a few steps before glancing back at me. Her brows arched. "Aren't you coming?"

The room the nurse takes us to is small. A lone exam table, a small sitting chair tucked in the corner, and a counter of medical supplies.

Pregnancy diagrams hang on the walls next to pictures of smiling babies.

"If you'll have a seat," the nurse instructs Sutton, "I'll ask you some questions before the doctor comes in."

I offer to take Sutton's bag and she scootches on the exam table, crinkling paper and all. She laughs. "I feel like a little kid with my legs dangling over the side."

I could live for her smiles.

"Alright, Miss Boyd." The nurse settles into the stool in front of the computer. "I see you filled out your online forms, but there are still some things I have to ask."

"Go for it."

Trying not to listen to her medical history, I pull out my phone and text Grant. I dropped Tristen off with him after school so I could get to the appointment on time. He didn't ask why I needed him to watch him, he simply told me to bring him by. Cole's still getting settled with the nanny he hired, and I don't want to add Tristen to the mix.

"What's your sexual history? Are you sexually active?"

My ears perk up.

Sutton glances uneasily over at me. "Yes."

Keys clack. "And are you using protection?"

I'm wondering if I should step out of the room.

"We were," she clears her throat, "but here we are." Her cheeks turn a lovely shade of rose as she laughs off her uneasiness.

We had used condoms that night. Multiple. But things happen. As it turns out, expiration dates are pretty important.

The nurse seems unfazed. "Are you in a relationship? Married?"

Sutton's feet thump against the table, her legs kicking with nerves. "Uh, single."

"Alright." More clicking of the mouse as the nurse ticks boxes on the screen. "The first day of your last menstrual cycle?" Sutton narrows her eyes, glancing towards the ceiling.

Shit. I'm glad I don't get all these questions when I go to the doctor. She gives an answer I don't catch.

Click. Click. "Alright," the nurse says. "Why do you think you're pregnant?"

"Well, I took an at-home pregnancy test. It came back positive." Sutton glances down at her clasped hands. "My roommate's a nurse and she asked questions that made me think I might be. Which is why I took the test."

More typing. "And what is the date of conception, if you know?"

I focus back on when we met. Cole had been giving me shit about being stressed out. Hell, both he and Grant had been. Grant offered to watch Tristan...

"June fifteenth," she says with full confidence. I quirk an eyebrow at her and she shrugs. "I was celebrating graduating college."

Oh fuck. I knew she was young, but I didn't expect her to be in her early twenties. What was I thinking?

Right. I was thinking there was a beautiful woman that I couldn't keep my eyes off of. How I wanted to walk across the room and introduce myself and get to see that beautiful smile up close. The goal was to get to know her. Not knock her up.

The kind nurse stands and hands Sutton a medical cup. "We'll need a urine sample. You can use the restroom down the hall. Put the sample in the slot when you're done. I'll leave a gown here for you," she gestures toward the exam table. "You'll need to undress from the waist down so the doctor can check everything."

Sutton hops down, taking the cup. "I know the drill. Thanks."

When she returns from the restroom, I step out into the hallway to give her some privacy. Everything is familiar, yet utterly different. When Sara was pregnant, I was just starting the landscaping business and missed appointments. Looking back, I wish I would've made more. Maybe then Tristan would've grown up with a mother.

Which is why I told Sutton that I want to be at every appointment, if she's okay with it. I don't think I could stand not knowing what's going on with my child growing in her belly.

"Penny for your thoughts?" Sutton peers at me through the crack in the door.

I push off the wall. "Only a penny? I think they're worth more than that."

She snorts. "Undoubtedly. You can come in, but can you give me a second to sit down first? This gown is completely open in the back."

Although I wouldn't mind seeing her rounded ass again, I nod. "Just give me a shout when you're ready."

After a muffled "come in," I take my seat in the corner. Sutton sits on the table, her hands clasped in her lap, legs kicking anxiously, a nervous look on her face. This can't be easy for her. Hell, it's difficult for me, and I'm not the one on the exam table.

Doors close in the hall. Voices murmur through the wall, the other patients chatting with the nurse or each other. I can't stand the silence. "What was your major?"

Her lips pop open with a click. "Psychology. I'm working at an office in town on an internship before my master's courses at the University of Indianapolis start."

"That's," I pause, trying to find the right words, "impressive."

She gives me a shy smile. "It'll be more impressive once I'm a licensed therapist. For now, though, I'm focusing on my classes hoping I don't fail out of my scholarship."

"Don't sell yourself short. You've clearly worked hard to get where you are."

"Thanks." She falls silent, her head drooping to look at her feet. "What do you do? I have a vague idea from the night we met, but..."

"You don't remember much?" I laugh.

"Right."

We'd had several drinks that night. I found her enchanting. It was like all the lights reflected off her skin. Her smile was the sun, drawing me to her warmth. She could've muttered utter nonsense, and I'd hang on every word. Completely enamoured.

She'd been the same. It was like that bar that night was meant only for us. The only purpose it served was to bring the two of us together.

We danced. Drank. And when lingering touches weren't enough, we found a darkened corner to spend time in until we left for more privacy.

I assumed I remember more from that night than she did. I had only just walked into the bar when I spotted her. There's no telling how long she and her friend had been there.

"I own a landscaping company. Green's Lawn and Landscaping." My small start up has grown since I started it the summer before my senior year of college. The business courses I took weren't teaching me anything I didn't already know, plus business took off faster than I expected. Sara wanted me to stick with school, finish out my degree before going all in on my business, but I didn't see the point.

Sutton chuffs. "And you think I'm impressive. That company does sound familiar."

It should. We got a contract with the city of Briar Springs to upkeep the local parks. Not to mention the work we do for the locals. Our fleet of trucks is all over the city, especially during the warmer months.

Three small raps on the door startle us. Sutton jumps, placing her hand over her heart, laughing as the doctor steps in.

"I didn't mean to scare you." A young woman in a white lab coat steps into the room, shutting the door behind her. A long ponytail slips off her shoulder. She's around my age, and I wonder if Grant is familiar with her. Maybe I could ask him some questions once I get the balls to share all this with him. There's nothing wrong with a young doctor, they're just inexperienced.

Inexperience can cost everything.

Sutton waves her off. "You're fine. I'm just jumpy."

She politely shakes both of our hands as she introduces herself. "It's nice to meet you both. I'm Doctor Arnold, but you can call me Doctor Diana, or just Diana." Sutton nods politely. "Well," Diana sits down on the stool, turning to face Sutton. "Congratulations. You're pregnant."

Sutton snorts. "Nice to know my constant throwing up isn't for no reason."

Has she been sick? She never mentioned it.

Doctor Diana smiles sympathetically. "It should die down here within the next couple of weeks." She checks the computer screen. "Based on the conception date you gave, you're right around ten weeks. Estimated due date is around mid-March, but I don't want to give a solid date just yet." She goes on, giving information about what to expect in pregnancy. Then she says something I wasn't expecting. "Want to see your baby?"

Fear and anxiety fill my chest. It feels as if all the air is sucked from the room. It's one thing to comprehend that I'm going to be a father again, but to physically see the baby growing in Sutton's belly?

Unbelievable.

Both women seem unfazed, chatting while Sutton arranges herself in the stirrups. Diana readies the internal sonogram wand.

I've seen this process before, and the second time around isn't any easier. That damn wand is frightening to look at, and knowing it's going inside Sutton makes me cringe.

Hell, she's as nervous as I am about this. She's just handling it better.

"Alright," Diana says, turning the monitor towards us. There, on the screen in black and white, is our baby.

Like a moth drawn to the flame, I push myself up from my seat to place a hand on Sutton's shoulder.

"That's my baby?" she asks, her voice thick with emotion.

Diana smiles. "It sure is. Want to hear the heartbeat?" With the click of a button, the rapid whooshing of our baby's heartbeat fills the room.

Sutton sucks in a ragged breath, her hand reaching up to clasp mine on her shoulder. Neither one of us dares to ruin this moment with words. Instead, we stare at the monitor, our healthy baby filling the screen, holding on to one another.

Chapter Four

Sutton

The cool plastic of the toilet seat feels like heaven against my hot cheek. Clammy sweat peppers my skin and my muscles shake. I spit out the reminisce of bile from my mouth, my stomach still issuing spasms of revolt. Convinced the worst has subsided, I curl up in a ball against the soothing cold of the bathroom floor. Not exactly the best place to be, but I couldn't give a shit right now.

For three weeks, the morning sickness has only gotten worse, not better. Ever since my appointment, I've been telling myself, *just a few more weeks, and it'll be over*. Maybe it's wishful thinking, but they flit through my head even now as my stomach rolls.

I barely make it to the bowl before what's left of my meager breakfast makes its reappearance.

Being pregnant is *miserable*.

I don't understand how there are women basking in the glow of pregnancy. All I've known is sickness. Miserable, vomit-y sickness. I'm a constant shade of pale green, which is impressive with my naturally tan skin.

What they fail to tell people is that "morning sickness" doesn't mean you only get sick *in the morning*. It's all damn day. A sip of coffee? Oh, no you don't. Boring toast? Think again. Plain rice for dinner? Not plain enough. Brushing my teeth? Game over.

I'm constantly puking my guts up. So much so that I don't know if I'll have the strength to get off this floor. I can call Kelly, but she's at work helping other sick people. She's been working toward getting her critical care qualifications, so all she does is work.

It's gotten so bad that I've had to call in sick to work. I've told no one aside from my family that I'm pregnant—it didn't go well. So for now, I'm keeping it a secret.

Dad got eerily silent, his mouth a thin, tight line on his face while he silently seethed. Mom demanded I come home to stay with them.

There's *no way* I'd give up my scholarship, move across states, and live with their silent disappointment. Not to mention, my baby's father and brother are here.

Wells.

Maybe I can call Wells to come and help me get back to bed. I'm sure it's not what he meant when he said he'd be with me every step of the way, but I don't have a lot of options at the moment, unless I want to stay on the bathroom floor all day.

We finally exchanged numbers before my doctor's appointment and he's been checking in to see how I'm doing. Not only is he hot, but he's kind too. I'm sure he wouldn't mind picking me up off the ground.

Time passes as I debate the pros and cons of calling for help. Several times, I attempt to push myself up, only to get nauseous and fall back to the floor in a heap. There's no way around it.

Using what little strength I have left, I grab my phone from where it rests on the edge of the tub and search for Wells' number. I put the call on speaker, too weak to hold it up to my ear.

It rings twice before he picks up. "Sutton? Is everything okay?"

This whole situation makes me want to laugh. I let out a weak chuckle instead. "No."

"Where are you? I'm on my way." There's no hesitation in his voice. In fact, all I hear is determination.

I look up at the white ceiling. "On the bathroom floor in my apartment."

Wells curses. "Give me your address. Do I need to call an ambulance? Are you hurt?"

Maybe I should've started with something less panic inducing.

He doesn't interrupt me as I list off my address, telling him where to find the spare key. Somehow, I convinced him not to call for an ambulance. "It's not that serious. I've had terrible morning sickness and feel too weak to get up, and Kelly isn't here."

"I'm right around the corner. I'll be there in a minute." He issues another order to stay put, and I can't help but roll my eyes. Of course, I'm not going anywhere.

True to his word, the door creaks open minutes later.

"Sutton?" Heavy footsteps clunk down the hall. "Shit," he curses, pushing open the bathroom door.

Wells cups my face, brushing hair off my clammy skin before checking me over for any injuries.

"I'm fine," I repeat. "I just need help getting up."

"You're *not* fine," he says sternly, his handsome face locked in a concerned scowl. Like I weigh nothing, Wells lifts me into his arms.

I'm having my very own damsel in distress moment, and even though I'm weak as hell, I'm living for it.

"My room's the second door on the left," I murmur, letting my head rest against his shoulder. Even though I'm sick, pregnant, and look like trash in a large sleep shirt I haven't taken off in days, fireworks ignite in my chest.

The same fireworks I felt the night we met.

Soft blankets hit my skin and I snuggle into them. A warm hand runs down my cheek. "Do you have food? Can you keep anything down?"

I swallow, tucking my hands under my chin. "Crackers should be in the cabinet next to the stove. I don't know if I'll keep them down, but I can try."

Warm, soft lips press against my temple. At least, I think they do. It's such a quick thing that I can't be positive it actually happened. By the time I crack an eye open, all I see is Wells' back as he goes on his search.

Normally I'd be embarrassed about how the apartment looks, but right now, I don't care. With Kelly working all the time and me battling the never ending morning sickness, things have gotten a bit out of hand.

Cabinets open and close in the kitchen. Like a soft melody, the racket somehow comforts me. My eyes grow heavy with exhaustion, and I stifle a yawn.

"Let's sit you up." The sound of Wells' warm voice and soothing touch has my eyes peeling open. "I found crackers and some ginger ale. Having something in your stomach should help."

I groan. "Trying to put something in my stomach got me in this situation."

Wells says nothing. He simply holds out a cracker and waits. The look in his green eyes is soft, yet determined. Then I remember he has a five-year-old, so this is an everyday type of event.

Knowing I'm fighting a losing battle, I relent, taking the offered cracker.

He waits for me to swallow before handing me ginger ale. "Does this happen a lot? I know you said at the doctor's office that you had morning sickness. I would've been doing more if I knew it was this bad."

I'm not sure how he could do more than he already is. His check-ins are nice. I often think of all the pregnant people who don't have this kind of support from the other parent involved. I honestly feel lucky to have someone like Wells. I couldn't have picked anyone better if I knew what I was getting myself into that night.

Bubbles pop and fizz down my throat. "It didn't start out this bad. Mostly it came and went, but now? I can't stop throwing up. I don't know what I would've done if you didn't answer the phone."

A crease forms between his eyebrows. "Sutton, I'll always answer. Here," he takes the can of soda from me in exchange for another cracker. "Where's your friend? Kelly?"

"Working."

"And you were here by yourself?" I nod my head. Something flashes behind his eyes before he looks away. "How long were you down there?"

I can't hide the cringe on my face. Even if I could, I have a feeling he'd notice it.

"Sutton, how long were you on your bathroom floor?"

Worry has overtaken his handsome face. As if he can't stop himself, he brushes a strand of hair out of my face, his rough hands gently caressing my skin. I want to melt into him. Want him to pull me into his chest like I was when he carried me in here. An overwhelming feeling to have him take care of me slides through me.

"You won't like the answer." My mouth goes dry, and it's not from the crackers.

His voice is soft and pleading. "Tell me anyway."

I shrug. "A couple hours, maybe? I wasn't really keeping track."

All he does is shake his head in frustration. Those green eyes focused on my face dance as something akin to determination settles in them. "It won't happen again."

Confusion has me furrowing my brow. "What does that mean?" I say around a mouth full of dry crackers.

Wells pushes himself off the bed, standing like a tower over me. "Eat," he says before wandering down the hallway.

Chapter Five

Wells

This can't happen again.

Frenetic energy builds under my skin. I *have* to do something. Anything to help this feeling of utter helplessness go away.

Sara always said I couldn't sit still.

I start with cleaning the bathroom. All I could picture is how long she was stuck on the floor. How she was curled in the fetal position in the small space.

She deserves to have someone taking care of her.

I want to take care of her. *Need* to take care of her.

The thought grows and grows until it's a living thing inside my head.

It's what keeps me here.

Once the bathroom is clean, I check on her. She's sleeping peacefully in her bed, cracker crumbs speckling her cheeks.

This woman is carrying my child.

Will they have green eyes or brown? Will their hair be the same shade of black as their mothers?

A lock clicks down the hallway. Keys clack against ceramic as someone comes through the front door. A female voice lets out a soft curse. "What the hell happened here? Sutton?"

Not wanting to wake her, I shut the bedroom door. "She's sleeping," I whisper.

A familiar scrub clad woman squints at me. "You better be the baby daddy, otherwise I'm pepper spraying your ass." She reaches into her bag, her threat ringing true.

"Whoa." I hold my palms up. "It's Wells. You're Kelly, right?" Her eyes narrow. "Sutton called me. She was stuck on the bathroom floor for hours, too weak to sit up. I helped her into bed and took care of her. Cleaned the bathroom, too."

Kelly scans the living room with an arched brow.

"And the rest of the apartment."

Suspicion falls from her face and she sighs. "She was on the floor for *hours*?"

I nod, lowering my hands. "She wouldn't tell me exactly how long, but yeah."

"Dammit, Sutton." Kelly tosses her purse on the floor before sinking onto the couch. She looks completely exhausted.

"Has she been like this the whole time?" I ask, sitting in a threadbare chair.

Kelly rubs her eyes. "I know she wouldn't want me to tell you, but yeah, pretty much." She points a finger at me. "I'm only telling you because I love that girl. She's stubborn and says she's fine, but she's not."

I nod.

Maybe the idea that's been marinating in my head isn't as crazy as I thought.

"I'm going to say goodbye. I've got to pick my son up from school." I stand, pulling my wallet from my pocket. "Here's my card. Please call me if she's sick again?"

Kelly takes the business card. "Again?" she scoffs. "Sutton's constantly sick these days."

I don't like that.

A sharp exhale slips from my lips. I'm frustrated at this whole situation. Frustrated that she's going through this right now. Frustrated that I can't be with her when she needs someone.

Needs *me*.

Sutton rolls over the second I slip through her door. Big brown eyes blink slowly, the sleep slipping away from them.

"Feel better?"

She stretches, letting out an adorable squeak. "How long was I out?"

I shrug, fighting a smile. "A couple hours."

Sutton snorts. "I see what you did there." She takes a hesitant sip from the ginger ale on her bedside table.

I gesture to the foot of her bed, sitting as she nods permission.

It's now or never.

I inhale sharply. "I wanted to offer you something, and you don't have to say anything right now. I'd like it if you came to live with me. The thought of you helpless on that bathroom floor..." I shake my head, angry that she's been in that position. "I want to take care of you. I know it's not expected, and maybe not even wanted, but my door's open."

Time will only help to learn the minute expressions that filter across her face, and I can't wait for the day when I can know what she's thinking by a single look. But right now, I'm not sure what the slant of her eyebrows mean, or the meaning behind the slight purse of her lips, and what the small sigh means.

"Thank you for showing up for me today. I probably would've been stuck there all day." She forces a laugh, as if it will help lighten the truth of her words. "Ahem, anyway. Thanks for the offer. I'll think about it."

I leave with the promise that she'll call me when she needs anything.

That's all I can ask for.

Chapter Six

Sutton

Potato chips crunch obnoxiously. "I think you should live with him." Kelly pops another chip into her already full mouth.

We've been bumming out on the couch, Gilmore Girls style, with bowls of salty, sweet, and relatively unhealthy foods spread before us. They're mostly for Kelly. They're *all* for Kelly, but she nearly bit my head off when I pointed out that I'll be munching on saltines and clear fizzy drinks.

Our couch isn't large enough for the two of us to lie down, so my feet rest on the back while Kelly's hang off the edge next to my elbow. A handmade knit blanket, courtesy of Kelly's grandma, drapes across us. It's a crazy way to relax, but it's one we've perfected through years of friendship.

"I don't know," I groan, pulling the blanket over my face, earning a complaint from Kelly.

The last two weeks have been just as bad. Maybe worse because I had to toughen it out at work. Wells, to his credit, has called me every afternoon. It's clockwork at this point.

He's been so good to me. Granted, he's one half of the reason I'm in this particular predicament, so I think I deserve his concern.

Kelly tugs on the blanket, dislodging her bag of chips. "What's not to know? Seriously, Sutton. I'm barely here, and when I am, it's usually spent sleeping or studying. You've been having a helluva time with blob—"

I point a finger at her. "Don't call my baby *blob*."

"—and honestly, Wells seems like a good guy. I mean, it's rare you find one as hot as he is who doesn't have an underlying dickhead symptom."

"First," I scoff, "*someone* sounds like they're projecting."

Crunch. "I'm not."

I roll my eyes and a chip hits my face. "You totally are."

My very sophisticated, mature roommate sticks her chip laden tongue out at me. Being equally mature, I return the favor.

"Second, I *barely* know the man. What is this, *The Real World*? I didn't sign up to be picked to live in a house with a stranger... I'm just knocked up by one."

"I mean," she sits up, switching out the chips for a drink. "You might as well get to know the man you're having a baby with. Plus, he's done all this before, right?" She waves at my stomach. "Don't get me wrong, I did my obstetrics rotation, but there's a reason I don't work in labor and delivery."

"Because a certain doctor doesn't work there?" I wiggle my brows.

Kelly laughs. "Shut up."

We both know exactly what I'm talking about. She's denying it, but I know.

I sigh. She's probably thinking the same thing about me right now.

Even though I won't admit it, I need more help than Kelly can offer right now. She's right. She's been so busy with everything at work that, although she tries, she can't be here for me all the time. The bathroom fiasco wasn't the first time and it won't be the last. My belly will only get bigger and that will open up a whole new can of worms.

Kelly grabs the Peanut Butter M&M's, popping a handful into her mouth, barely chewing before saying, "Spit it out. I know what that face means."

"What face? I'm not making a face."

She holds the bag of sweet candies out to me. I know they'll probably have me running for the bathroom, but I need a sweet treat right about now. Chocolate and peanut butter coat my tongue, and I revel in its sweetness before the revolt begins. "Ugh, fine. Maybe you're right."

She sucks in a mocking gasp. "It's a miracle."

"Blob is only going to get bigger."

"Ha, I knew it would catch on."

"Things are only going to get more difficult and I can't do it myself." Kelly issues a complaint. "I know you'll help as much as you can. But like you said, you can't be around all the time." I suck in a deep breath. "Also, you've got your own stuff to worry about."

Kelly's mouth hangs open. "So you're gonna do it? You'll move in with him?"

Fear of the unknown slices through me. Since I moved away from home, I've lived with Kelly. She's my best friend, my support system. I'm not sure I can do it without her. A tear trickles down my cheek.

"No, don't do that." Kelly tosses the bag aside, wrapping me in a comforting hug. "Shhh. You're gonna do great."

"What will I do without you?" I sniffle.

Kelly laughs, her body shaking mine. "You're not losing me, Sutton. Think of it this way." She pulls back, wiping tears from my cheeks. "You'll be gaining so much more. Plus, I think Wells is nicer to look at than me. And I think he might be smitten with you."

I scoff. "Yeah right."

"Trust me, babe. The man has hearts for eyes. And if he hurts you," she says in a sweet voice, "I'll gouge his eyes out."

IT'S BEEN A LONG DAY at work. I'm exhausted and hungry, and all I want to do is fall into bed. Which is what I'd be doing if I wasn't moving in with Wells tonight.

Every day, I flip-flop on my decision. I'm not going through something that no other pregnant person has gone through before. It'll go away eventually. But I'm struggling. Part of me doesn't want anyone to take care of me, but, admittedly, I need it. Wells is a stranger, yes, but he's already dropped everything to make sure I'm okay. I'm not doing this for myself. I'm doing it for my baby.

Plus, there's something between Wells and I, and I'm not strong enough to resist it.

After a week of packing, unbidden tears, and countless unspoken worries, it's finally time. No matter how you argue it, Kelly's right.

Wells gave an audible sigh of relief when I called to tell him I was taking him up on his offer. I could practically see the smile on his face as we made plans for our new living arrangements.

This time, when I pull up to Wells' house, the backseat of my car is full of bags containing my meager possessions. Boxes roll around in the trunk, bumping and rattling on my silent drive.

He's waiting for me. Sitting on his porch wearing worn-out jeans and a black t-shirt, looking every bit as tempting as he did the first time. His son, Tristan, runs around the yard kicking a soccer ball and wiping sweat from his forehead. He's so *little*. So small compared to what a five-year-old should be.

Will my baby look like him? Will they share the same smile?

Wells waves, his smile breaking across his face like the sunrise. Maybe Kelly was right, and he has hearts for eyes.

Shit, if she knew how often I think about how right she is, she'd throw a party. Better keep this one to myself.

Tristan beats him to the car. "Are you my dad's friend?"

I chuckle, smiling down at his red face. "We can say that."

"Yes, she's my friend. I told you she's staying with us, remember?"

Tristan looks between me and Wells, his brows furrowed in confusion. "Is she why there're sheets on the couch?"

We both laugh.

"Yes," Wells says to his son before looking at me. "For me."

I nod because what else is there to do?

The house is like a dream, all blurry and hazy. This is where he tossed his keys the second we were inside. I graze the light blue walls with a finger. This is where he pushed me against the wall, where his hands slid up my thighs, where I felt how much he desired me, wanted me, *needed* me.

Very real heat tingles down my spine and I blink rapidly, trying to clear the images from my head. How I can swing from mildly nauseous like always to unbearably horny is enough to give me whiplash. Damn pregnancy hormones.

"You okay?" Wells' brows furrow. "You're flushed."

Uh-oh. I've been caught. "Um, no. I mean, I'm fine." I rub my forehead to hide the lie in my eyes.

The way his moss gaze lingers on me makes me think he remembers, too. That he sees the same visions of that night dancing in his mind, too.

Wells clears his throat before leading me down the hallway. There's no need for him to tell me where we're going. I already know.

His room is plain. Simple. Clean. I only saw it shrouded in darkness. Only saw *him* that night.

A closet door that doesn't quite latch sits opposite the bed, a tiny bathroom tucked in the corner next to it. Hues of golden sunset flicker through the white curtains on the far side of the room, a dresser resting underneath it.

"Half the closet is yours and I've cleared out the top two shelves on the dresser. Sorry, I don't have more space for you."

"Seriously? This is fine. More space than I had in my bedroom. I should be the one that's sorry for the mess you had to see." I chuckle, looking at my feet. "Thank you. For cleaning. And now."

A firm hand tilts my chin up. Warmth. That's what I feel when he looks at me. Warmth and adoration, but there's something veiled that I can't quite figure out. "You're welcome, Sutton."

Oh, boy. I'm in so much trouble.

Chapter Seven

Wells

It's late by the time we get home. Much later than I wanted it to be. All day there's been an itch to get home. To get to *her*.

Sutton's compact car sits in the driveway, slivers of light slipping through the blinds of the living room. A sense of relief fills my chest at the mere thought of her, safe and warm.

Tristan's cleats clack on the concrete of the porch.

"Put your ball up and get ready for a bath. You stink." My son's blonde hair runs through my fingers. He's so much like his mother, it almost hurts.

His face scrunches. "I don't stink."

"Yes, you do." I hold the door open for him. "I'm surprised you haven't made the flowers die."

"Flowers don't die from stink," he laughs.

Jeopardy plays softly on the tv, shades of blue flickering across the living room. "They do when stinky boys come home from soccer practice."

Sutton lies in a curled up heap on the couch, a blanket wrapped around her as she sleeps, her laptop stacked on top of textbooks.

Tristan kicks his ball across the room, making it bounce down the hallway. "Oops." His big green eyes echo how sorry he is. He knows not to kick the ball in the house.

The sternness of my expression speaks for itself. "Go. Now." I whisper to not wake sleeping beauty.

Small feet clomp down the hall, and I sigh, letting the exhaustion from the way weigh me down.

I missed a doctor's appointment.

In the three weeks Sutton's lived with us, not one day went by without her being sick. Harsh shadows rest under her tired eyes, the glow of her skin dulling each day. She's lost weight too.

I lower myself to the end of the couch, careful not to wake her. The knots in my back pull, making me wince as I drag a hand down my face. I'm not as young as I used to be and sleeping on an old couch at thirty years old is taking its toll. Maybe buying a shitty mattress and sleeping on the floor of Tristan's room would be better than this.

Sutton moves, a small whimper slipping from her lips in sleep. Even now she can't get away from it. It kills me that the woman carrying my child is suffering. Even worse is that there's nothing but words of comfort that I can give her.

I reach for her, stroking her blanket clad shin. I only allow myself small touches to comfort her. Rubbing her back while she vomits, brushing a cool washcloth along her face and neck, holding back thick black hair for her when she doesn't have time to do it herself. Carrying her to my bed and wrapping her in blankets.

These are the things I know to do, and it's still not enough. There's no calling my best friend for advice on what to do to make it better. He's a damned pediatrician.

Sutton stirs again, this time yawning and blinking her eyes open. "Hey."

"Did you know you're the only person I know who watches Jeopardy?" I won't ask the one question I really want to ask. There's no point. We've reached the point in our cohabitation that I can at least tell when she's frustrated, and right now, she hates being asked how she's feeling.

She'll lie anyway and we both know it.

Sutton snorts, rubbing at her eyes. "It's more a comfort than anything. Growing up, my dad would watch it and I'd sit in his lap while he guessed wildly at the answers." She laughs, a hand falling to her stomach and rubbing gentle circles.

A smile pulls at my lips.

Tristan comes running in wearing nothing but his underwear, with two sets of pajamas in his hands. "Which ones should I wear, Sutton?"

Her smile is breathtaking.

My son's loving having someone else in the house. Sutton takes it all in stride, not bothered by anything he does. Their most recent game, if we can call it that, has been picking out his nightly jammies.

Sutton grimaces as she sits up, but quickly replaces it. "Hmm, let's see what you've got."

Tristan holds up a green dinosaur set, followed by a yellow set with construction equipment. Both are hand-me-downs from Harrison and Jett. He's so much smaller than them that, although they're the same age, Tristan fits into their outgrown clothes.

"Oh, both are excellent choices." She holds a delicate finger to her chin in contemplation. "I think...the green one. It goes with your eyes."

Tristan issues a quick *thanks* and takes off down the hallway.

"I'll be there in a minute to start your bath," I call after him.

Sutton runs a hand down her small bump. "He's fun."

"Can be." I lean forward, running a hand through my hair. I can't put my question off any longer. "How'd your appointment go?"

Kelly and I had worked hard on getting Sutton to call her doctor. She wanted to put it off until she was out of the first trimester, saying that the morning sickness would go away. Well, she's nearing fifteen weeks now, past her first trimester, and the morning sickness isn't letting up.

Sutton sighs. "Basically, it's just terrible morning sickness. Not enough to warrant a diagnosis, but she put me on some nausea meds to help. I have the paperwork if you want to look at them later. We should

49

get the blood screening results by the end of the week, and then we'll go back in a couple of weeks after that for the anatomy scan."

I nod. "I'm sorry I couldn't be there today."

She knows how important it is for me to be there, for her and our baby. When the doctor's office called to see if she could come in a couple of days early, I told her not to wait. Her well being is more important than my ability to go with her.

"I know you wanted to be there," she breathes. The ghost of her hand along my back has me sucking in a stolen breath. It's been difficult keeping my touches to myself. Feeling her hand on my back is the opposite of relaxing. "You'll be at the next one." She chuckles to herself. "I'm picturing you plowing through anyone that gets in your way."

I snort. "You're not wrong."

"That truck of yours would do some damage."

How can she pull a smile from me so easily?

"Dad!"

"Uh-oh, someone's impatient," Sutton says, her hand sliding off my sore back.

Tristan's scrubbed clean of the sweat and dirt from soccer practice and chasing Harrison and Jett at the playhouse after dinner and is tucked safely in his bed.

Sutton's no longer lounging on the couch, the tv blank and silent. A pang of regret hits my chest at the same time as a muscle in my back twinges. It's right under my shoulder blade, too far for me to reach myself. I roll my shoulders, hoping to loosen the ache before fixing my bed for the night.

"You know, I don't think I've ever slept on a couch as uncomfortable as that one." The pop of the refrigerator door comes from the kitchen.

I smile at the offending piece of furniture. "It's seen better days. It was second-hand when we bought it." Sara insisted on stopping at the estate sale. There wasn't much left except for tiny trinkets and this old couch.

A bottle cap twists open behind me and I find Sutton standing by the dining room table in her blue slippers. Like a moth drawn to the flame, my eyes scan up her tan legs, over her hips, and to her face. She's tied up her thick black hair like she does when she's getting ready for bed, showcasing her beautiful face.

I could stare at her all day.

"Makes me wonder how you sleep on it every night."

I sigh, turning back to the couch and tossing my pillows down. "Would you believe me if I said I sleep like a baby?"

She snickers. "Absolutely not. I took a nap on that thing and already feel sore."

"The floor is almost preferable."

"I'll keep that in mind next time. In my experience, floors can be quite nice. Especially if the tile is cool and your skin is warm and clammy. Highly recommend." She laughs at my stern expression. "It had me thinking though."

I quirk an eyebrow. "Yeah?"

The bottle in her grip crinkles. "It's not right for me to come here and displace you—"

"You're not."

"It's your house." She gives a soft smile. "I don't feel right taking up your space. And now that I know what it's like to sleep on *that*," she points to the couch. "I know your back has to be killing you."

She's not leaving. She *can't* leave.

I don't want her to leave.

"It's fine." I'll sleep on this shitty fucking couch for the rest of my life if it meant she wouldn't leave.

She sighs, rolling her eyes as if exasperated. "What I'm *trying* to say is that your bed is big enough for both of us. What kind of person would I be to let you suffer while I only take up half the bed?"

My head shakes automatically. "You don't have to do that. I'm fine out here."

"My god," she laughs, throwing up her hands. "Get off your high horse and come sleep with me." Her eyes widen as if realizing what she's said. "Not like that. I mean sleep, not... *sleep*."

She's so fucking cute.

The offer is tempting. More than tempting, really. I glance down the hall to my son's bedroom door. How confusing will it be for him?

Fuck, this whole thing has been confusing for him.

Sutton's soft whisper breaks through the loudness of my thoughts. "Please. It's the least I can do."

Maybe it's the tone of her voice, the gentle pleading lying underneath her words. Maybe it's the feeling I have when she's near. Or, it could be the unceasing pinching of the muscles of my back that has me nodding in agreement.

Hours later, she's tucked under the covers on the side of the bed she's claimed as her own. She's not sleeping, I can tell that much.

"What, no fort of pillows to distinguish boundaries?"

Sutton hisses a laugh. "I think we're past that, don't you? Considering I'm pregnant with your baby and all."

For the first time in weeks, a soft mattress hits my back. Bones crackle as I adjust my sleeping position, letting out small sighs of relief.

"Damn Wells," she laughs, rolling over to face me. "Exactly how old are you? I'm beginning to think you're much older than you look."

Her playful tone brings a smile to my face. "Ancient, apparently."

Sutton smiles, her eyes glinting in the dim lamplight. "I knew it."

Chapter Eight

Sutton

Like clockwork, I wake before Wells' alarm. It's become a habit now. Each morning I wake with his arm draped across my hip, his hand cradling my growing baby bump. Wells is sound asleep, his warm breath tickling my neck.

It's my favorite time of the day. My perfect, iridescent bubble of warmth.

More often than not, we find our way to each other during sleep. At first, I was self-conscious of how close I'd get to him, not wanting to cross an invisible boundary. But now, I don't bother fighting it.

I crave his touch.

Thanks to the medication, my nausea has dulled, only occasionally sending me sprinting to the nearest toilet. But now this *need* has taken over me.

From what the books say, it's because of the crazy flood of hormones. But I think it's Wells. His smell, his gentle touches. Even the way he looks at me sends embers of heat through me.

It's strange. I know what it feels like to have his skin on mine. I know the sounds he makes when he sinks into me. Those memories are like a plague now, killing me slowly as the ache grows.

Wells murmurs something in his sleep, pulling me closer to him. His fingers flex on my stomach, sending shivers down my spine.

Is this torture? Oh, definitely. Would I give it up for anything in the world? Absolutely not.

I itch to run my fingers through his hair, to hold him against me, but I don't. It's not like he asked for his bed back. He was willing to sleep on that godforsaken piece of furniture for as long as I stayed here.

Hell, he might not even want my touch for all I know.

All too soon, the alarm blares. Wells hisses a curse, flinging himself to the nightstand beside him to silence it before it wakes me.

Bubble popped.

It's easy to feign sleep. Just close my eyes and listen as he gets ready for work. I don't need to see him to know that he's wearing black jeans, work boots, and his company's t-shirt. His hair still wet from his shower as he tosses on a jacket to combat the chilly fall morning. He'll wake up Tristan next, slowly getting him ready for the day before dropping him off at school.

I might feel like a creep, but the routine of it is comforting.

Some days, though, I feel like not pretending. I want to be a part of this early morning routine. I can't stop picturing it, really. What it would look like with me in it.

Would we shower together? Start the day with his hands on my body, washing my hair, kissing my neck. Would I help make Tristan's breakfast? Get Wells' thermos of coffee ready? Kiss him on his way out?

Instead of being plagued by sickness, today I'm plagued by rogue hormones. My nipples are sensitive, sending zings of pleasure when the fabric of my bra brushes against them. I can feel how badly my body is craving the one thing I can't have. Hell, even crossing my legs is uncomfortable in the best way.

I need some best friend advice. It's still early enough in the evening that Wells and Tristan aren't home yet. I slip my shoes off my feet and plop on the bed as the phone rings.

Kelly answers on the third ring. "Hey, momma, how you feelin'?"

"I have a question."

"Wow, Sutton, I'm so glad you feel amazing. Isn't pregnancy great? What was that? You miss me? Oh, honey, I miss you too. I have no one to judge me when shoving chips in my face." A distinct crunch follows a familiar rustle.

I shake my head, a ghost of a smile pulling at my lips. "You're ridiculous."

She clears her throat. "Okay, so now that we've gotten the pleasantries out of the way, what's your question?"

"It's a medical question."

Chip bags crunch on the other end. Kelly's tone turns serious. "Are you okay?"

"Technically, yes."

"Okay..."

I suck in a deep breath. "Is it normal to be horny all the damn time?"

Kelly laughs. "Sutton, you have an OBGY-N for a reason."

"I know, but this is personal."

"Pretty sure she's seen your coochie. Answering a horny-ness question is nothing."

Damnit, she's right.

"Will you just answer my question? I've been on edge all day and I need to know if it's because of my pregnancy or for other reasons."

She chuckles. "Like wanting to fuck your baby daddy?"

"I hate you."

Kelly's unfazed. "You love me. But, to answer your question, it could be both. If I remember correctly, your hormones throw everything off balance, increase blood flow to your downstairs, essentially making you want to hump anything that moves."

"Jesus, Kelly."

"But my non-medical brain is also thinking that you have the hots for Wells, which I completely understand."

I exhale heavily into the phone. "That's what I was afraid of."

"Blob making you horny or the Wells part?"

"I don't know. Both?" I know it's both, but it doesn't make it any less confusing. It's insane how my body responds to Wells. The very first night we met, it was hard to ignore. I wouldn't be pregnant right now if I had.

"You want to know what I think? I think you wanted me to tell you to have sex with Wells. I think you needed some assurance that this wasn't a bad or dirty thing to do. He's already knocked you up, so he should have no problem helping you with this. And if I know anything about baby daddy, it's that he would do anything for you."

She's right. Of course she's right. "Who was the psych major again?"

She laughs. "I don't need to have a degree in psychology to know what my best friend is thinking."

Doubt still taints the truth in her words. Wells cares for me. I just don't know if he *wants* me like he did. "So, what? I proposition him?"

"Of course you do! There's nothing wrong with two consenting adults...scratching an itch. Here's what you should do: sit him down tonight, tell him what you're thinking, and see what he says. If it's no, we can find you a good vibrator. A fancy one with all the settings."

I laugh, shaking my head. "You know from experience, huh?"

"Hey, don't judge me," she laughs. "A girl's gotta do what a girl's gotta do. And you gotta go do your sexy baby daddy."

TRISTAN WENT TO BED an hour ago.

All night I've been thinking about how to start his conversation, but is there really a good way to say, "Hey, I want you to fuck me like you did the night you knocked me up?"

I can picture his arched brow and confused expression. He'd definitely say no, right?

Even thinking about the possibility of him saying yes has wetness pooling between my thighs.

Wells sits on the couch in the living room with his computer on his lap. He spends most nights looking over the day's work or balancing the budget, creating mock-ups for potential clients.

Wells glances up at me as I step into the living room. "Hey."

I sit on the couch next to him. "Whatcha working on?"

"The city wants to create a rose garden in Maxwell park next summer. They're wanting to know what the general layout would be and a pricing estimate. If we're able to book this, it'll mean a boost in business." He sighs, turning his computer toward me.

The screen displays crisscrossing rows, creating a beautiful geometric design around a center circle. Wells opens another tab showcasing the roses that would work best in our climate.

"That's amazing." I've never ceased to be impressed by him. He owns a successful business while raising his son as a single dad.

And now there's me.

He sighs, closing his computer. "It'll be even more amazing once we sign a contract." Wells glances down at his watch. "Did you need something?"

Maybe tonight is a bad night. The last thing he needs is for me begging him to screw me. "No, it's fine. Not a big deal."

His eyes soften as he looks back at me. "You sure?" The way he studies my face has me squirming in my seat. Not because I'm turned on by him, because I am, but because of how exposed it makes me feel.

"Yeah," I say, pushing myself off of the couch, my hand falling to my growing stomach.

Wells places his hand over mine. It's not meant for me. It's a loving gesture from a father to their unborn child. But that doesn't stop my heart from racing.

I slip down the hallway with a quick goodnight, stopping to brush my teeth before sliding under the sheets.

It doesn't take long for Wells to follow after me. His footsteps are light as he steps into the bedroom, softly closing the bathroom door as he gets ready for bed.

When the bed dips from his weight, I turn towards him. "Hey."

Wells sighs. "I didn't mean to wake you."

"You didn't." The moonlight filtering through the curtains illuminates his profile. He's laying flat on his back, a hand resting on his chest.

I hear more than see his head nod. "Good."

Wells sighs again as he settles into the bed for sleep. But I'm not ready to sleep. I *can't* sleep. Not with this need crawling under my skin.

"Wells?" I breathe.

"Hmm?"

Here goes nothing. "Do you ever think about the night we met?"

Wells stills. If I could see his face clearly, I'd bet his eyes popped open. He doesn't even seem to breathe.

After what seems like an eternity, Wells rolls to face me. We're inches apart, close enough for me to make out his face. "Of course I do."

Hope takes off in my chest. "You do?"

Wells snorts, his lips turning up in a smile. "You're a walking reminder of that night, Sutton."

"Right. Growing baby bump." This isn't where I wanted this conversation to go. Maybe I should've stuck with Kelly's advice. I bet knocking his computer out of his lap and straddling him on the couch would've worked just fine. But now I'm trying to talk around what I actually want to say.

Wells' eyebrows furrow. Slowly, he lifts his hand, bringing it up to my cheek. "Say what you want to say, Sutton. You don't have to hide yourself from me."

The combination of the dark bedroom, his hand against my cheek, and our whispered conversation makes everything feel intimate.

My cheek flames underneath his palm. "I need you." The admission hangs in the space between us.

Wells brings his forehead to mine. "I'm here. I'm wherever you need me to be."

"No." I shake my head. "I *need* you."

He pulls back, his dark gaze searching mine in the moonlight. "What do you mean? I need to hear you say it."

This is mortifying.

Did I expect him to automatically roll himself on top of me and fuck me senseless? No.

Do I want him to? Abso-fucking-lutely.

I swallow, unable to speak the words he needs to hear.

Wells' voice is deep and rough. "If you want to know whether I want you, you haven't been paying attention. I've wanted you since I saw you. Dreamed of you for weeks after you left. Smelled your perfume in the air for days. Thinking about you drives me crazy. *You* make me crazy. So I need you to say it."

Hearing his admission sets my pulse pounding. I can feel how wet I'm getting from his simple words.

"I wasn't sure if you were open to rekindling that part of whatever it is that we are. Wells, I'm on fire for you. I ache for you." The words barely leave my mouth before he devours me with a soul-wrenching kiss.

To even think, for one second, that I forgot what it felt like to kiss Wells is impossible. He kisses me like he'll never kiss anyone again. He pours everything he won't say, can't say, in the caress of his lips, the flick of his tongue.

I clutch him to me, running my hands through his hair. Wells pushes me to my back, his delicious weight pressing me into the mattress. Small whimpers hum in my throat as his hands grip my waist, his leg parting mine. I gasp as his strong thigh presses against my pounding clit.

Wells moans. "I've missed that sound."

My hips rock against him, seeking friction. "Feels so good."

Wells' hand slides up my shirt, cupping my breast. Fingers softly trace my peaked nipple, and I arch into his touch, dizzy with need. My breath hitches as Wells shifts his thigh again, adding more pressure.

The proof of how much he wants me presses against my stomach. I slip my hand beneath the waistband of his shorts and wrap my fingers around him. Wells moans, his hips rocking into me. My pussy clenches and I ache with the need to be filled. "I want you inside me," I pant. "I want to feel you."

Wells kisses me before pulling away. The loss of his heat has goosebumps peppering my skin. A flash of rejection slashes through me before I realize he's locking the door. "We have to be quiet," he warns, ridding himself of his clothes.

His gaze never leaves mine as he undresses. Waves of anticipation and arousal flood through me. He's all mine.

Wells stands at the foot of the bed, heat burning in his eyes. He drags the comforter down my body inch by inch. I want to kick myself free of them, do anything to put his hands back on my body, but I'm frozen with anticipation.

Goosebumps pepper my skin as Wells runs his hands up my thighs, leaving scorching heat in their wake. In one smooth motion, he drags my shorts and panties down, tossing them to the side. Wells kneels between my thighs, continuing to graze his palms over my sensitive skin, up my torso. I sit up, giving him room to maneuver my shirt over my head until I'm naked before him. Wells doesn't hide the way his eyes take in all of me. They snag on my heavy breasts before dragging down between my spread thighs.

"Look at you. You're soaking." Wells reaches out, running a finger down my center.

"Wells, please." My hips rise to meet his hand.

He takes mercy on me, crawling up my body, kissing my belly before notching himself at my center. Delicious weight sinks me into the mattress. Wells braces himself on his elbows, his eyes locked on mine. "Remember, be quiet."

I'm so wet that Wells slides inside me in one smooth thrust. Breath leaves my lungs as I'm stretched by his cock. "Yes."

My pussy clenches around him. He's barely buried himself inside of me and I'm already balancing on the edge.

"Fuck, Sutton," he hisses. "You're so tight."

I raise my hips to meet his thrusts, burying him deeper. "You feel so good."

It's slow and deep and all-consuming. Nothing else matters except for this: his body moving as one with mine. Deep and slow.

It doesn't take long before the pleasure becomes too much. I'm panting, sweat coating my skin as I lose control. A firm hand covers my mouth, my moans growing louder. But I can't stop it. Can't stop my body from exploding in the most powerful orgasm I've ever experienced.

Wells curses as I pulse around him, my body bowing into his as I fall to pieces.

"One more," Wells commands. "I want to feel you come all over my cock one more time, Sutton. I'm not done with you yet." His hand slips down my body and over my sensitive clit. I writhe beneath him, my nipples brushing over the rough hair sprinkled on his chest. Wells thrusts harder, his breath growing ragged the closer he gets to his release. Our breath mingles, our eyes locked as I come again.

He groans as my pussy clenches around him. This time, I'm the one staunching his moans with my palm. Hot wetness coats my walls as his cock pulses inside me, spilling his release.

After several minutes in a bubble of bliss, Well rolls over on his side, his chest heaving. "That was even better than I remember," I say in a daze.

Next to me, Wells chuckles, a hand running through his messy hair. "Feel free to do that anytime." He leans on an elbow, cupping my face, and kissing me. "Don't forget how I feel about you." I nod, pulling him down to kiss me one more time before he rolls out of bed. "Let's shower."

Chapter Nine

Wells

The sound of my footsteps as I pace back and forth in the living room is the only sound in the house. Tristan's at Grant's for the night, and now I'm waiting.

Everything about Sutton and I is ass backwards. We're having a baby together. She's living with me. We're sleeping together. But I don't *know* her. Sure, I've started to learn the subtle nuances of her expressions, but there's so much more to her than the sigh she makes when I sink into her.

Fuck, I love that sound.

So tonight, I'm taking Sutton out on a date. It's been a long time since I've done this and I'm nervous as hell.

She should be home any minute. The classes she's taking at the University of Indianapolis meet every other week. Normally, she's home before I get here, working on assignments.

Sutton's working herself too hard.

The worrying thought refuses to leave, burrowing deeper into my psyche with every step. Her job, her class work, growing a baby, being sick all the damn time...she needs a break.

The past can't repeat itself. I won't be able to handle it.

Keys jangle and a second later, the lock clicks and Sutton steps inside. Arms laden with her bags and books and her giant metal water bottle, she glances at me and pauses. Her dark hair cascades over one shoulder, those brown eyes narrowing as they flit down my body at the slacks and button-up shirt I'm wearing. "What's going on?" she asks, crossing the room to set her things down on the table.

Having her here in the same room soothes my worried thoughts.

My hands slide into the front pocket of my pants, and I squeeze them into fists. "I wanted to take you out on a date, if you're up to it."

Sutton raises an eyebrow. "Are you sure, because you look a little tense," she says with a laugh.

I pull my hands from my pockets. "I'm sure."

Her hips sway in the loose dress she's wearing as makes her way to me. With our baby growing, her pants no longer fit, so she opts for more loose fitting dresses and skirts. She stops in front of me, her hands sliding up my chest to hook around my shoulders.

Her touch acts like a balm to my nerves, and I can feel myself relaxing. Breathing her in, I pull her closer. "Sorry. It's been awhile."

"Your mouth was saying one thing, but your body another." Fingers run through the hair on the back of my head before soothing down my neck. "I'd love to go on a date with you, Wells."

Relief floods through me, and before I can stop myself, her lips are against mine. Sutton clings to me, her arms wrapping tighter around my neck as mine wind around her waist. The kiss grows deeper, her lips parting in invitation. I groan as the taste of her nearly brings me to my knees.

This electric connection between us is something I've never experienced. It's addicting. All-consuming.

Sutton tenses, gasping against my lips, her hot breath caressing my skin.

Concern replaces the desire our kiss sparked. "What? What is it?"

Her wide brown eyes break away from mine to glance down the hallway. "Tristan," she whispers.

"Not here." I smile down at her surprised expression. "He's at Grants for the night."

Sutton smacks my chest, but that doesn't hide the amusement in her eyes. "Here I was, thinking we were breaking a cardinal rule. I almost had a heart attack thinking we were going to get caught."

"No heart attacks, please." I hold tighter to her, fighting against the image of her collapsing in my arms. I brush her hair away from her face. "How are you feeling? Any nausea?"

The medication Doctor Diana put her on has made a significant difference. Color is returning to her face, and she's looking more healthy. That glow people talk about is starting to take root.

"A little. It still comes and goes. It hit pretty hard around lunch, but thankfully it passed quickly. I ended up putting lunch back in the fridge after that."

"So you're hungry? We can't have that." The smile she gives me stops me in my tracks.

"Starving."

VANILLA ICE CREAM MELTS down the side of the waffle cone. Sutton makes a distressed squeal, her tongue flicking out to lap up the drizzle. "Why is it melting so fast?"

I'm captivated by the sight of her licking the cone, the creamy white treat coating her tongue. I'm mostly happy she's eating and enjoying her ice cream without getting sick, but I'm enjoying this too much. My dick twitches in my slacks and I look away, trying to get my racing heart under control.

It's always been like this with Sutton. This connection we have is unlike anything I've ever experienced. With each passing moment, I want her more. Need her more.

"Here." I tug the napkin off the end of my cone and hand it to her. "It's dripping down your hand."

"No!" she cries, hastily twisting her wrist and licking up the melting cream. "Help."

SIERRA SHIPLEY

I laugh, holding her wrist steady, swiping off what she missed with a napkin. "You're a mess."

She huffs a laugh. "I'm pretty sure that's well established at this point."

Street lights illuminate the gold streaks in her brown eyes. The chill of fall has settled into the air with the setting of the sun. Dinner was hit or miss, with Sutton scrunching her nose in disgust at the salmon she was craving. The steak on my plate, though, had her sighing with content the moment it hit her lips. I didn't mind swapping plates. Seeing her eating was more than enough sustenance.

The ice cream, though, was a pleasant surprise. She grabbed my arm, eyes going wide as we passed a locally owned creamery.

I can't say no to her.

"You're far from a mess. Maybe not right now," I laugh.

Sutton takes a giant bite off the tip of the ice cream, leaving teeth marks. She bends over, covering her mouth, laughing. "That was a bad idea," she mumbles. "It's cold."

"Okay, I think it's time to go home now," I laugh.

She nods her agreement, tossing her half-eaten ice cream into a nearby trash can. "Can't take me anywhere."

We walk side-by-side as we head back to my truck. Sutton's walking slower than usual, rubbing her belly as we walk. "Feeling okay?" I know she hates when I ask, but I can't help myself.

"All good. Just full." Her small hand grasps mine, squeezing it lightly. "Not only do I have a blob baby, but I'm also rocking a food baby."

I snort. "What the hell is a *blob baby*?"

"Okay, don't be mad, but it's kinda what Kelly and I call our baby."

"You...named our baby...blob?"

She snorts, pulling on my arm. "Of course not." She pauses. "Kelly did."

"And you went with it?" I say with a laugh.

66

"She's convincing when she wants to be. Think of blob as a short-lived term of endearment."

"Do I even want to know where she came up with this?" I'm not mad, I'm more intrigued.

She shrugs. "It was after our first ultrasound. Kelly was convincing me to live with you and it stuck."

"Blob, huh?"

"You've gotta admit it's catchy." Her grin is dazzling.

I shake my head. "I don't think I'll ever call our baby blob."

"Did you and Sara have a nickname for Tristan?" Her voice has gone soft. She knows I'm a widower. Hell, my wife's picture is all throughout our home, but she's not a subject I like to broach.

A lump forms in my throat. An image of Sara when she was pregnant lingers in my mind, so beautiful it hurts. She cradles her hands around our growing son as she smiles at me.

Sutton's never pressed me about Sara, and I'm thankful for that. But I know the time will come when I'll tell her what happened. Talk to her about the worst day of my life and pray like hell history doesn't repeat itself.

I clear my throat. "Um, she called him junior."

"Junior's cute. Why did blob have to stick? Now I can't get it out of my head. Wanna come up with something together?"

"You can call them blob. I'll just call them *ours.*"

Sutton sags dramatically against me, a hand resting over her heart. "God, you don't even try!"

In an instant, all the melancholy disappears. I lead her to a nearby bench, not wanting the night to end just yet. "What?"

The way she smiles at me, amusement lingering in her eyes, is all I need. "You're something else, Wells Green."

She doesn't hesitate when I lean over and kiss her. It's chaste, but it doesn't mask the desire behind it. "You're amazing, Sutton Boyd."

She scoffs. "I'm not too sure about that. I'm a pregnant twenty-three-year-old grad student."

"Why psychology? I don't think I ever asked."

Sutton fidgets with her fingers. "I've always liked the idea of helping people. Listening and being there through the good and bad. Noticing what's not being said and analyzing it. Understanding thought processes and figuring out a new way forward."

"Someone who loves all of that seems pretty amazing to me."

Sutton clears her throat as if embarrassed. "What made you want to start your own business?"

"My uncle has his own lawn company in Iowa. Every summer, my parents would ship me out there to work for him. He's the one that got me into landscaping. I still ask for advice now and then."

"So, you're close with your family?"

"Yeah." I take her hand in mine, rubbing circles on her soft skin.

We sit on the bench, talking and learning about each other. She's a skilled storyteller and has me laughing about her brother getting them lost in rural Missouri. Her family is tight-knit like mine, but they didn't respond well when she told them about the pregnancy.

"It was already hard enough to tell them, because I knew they'd be disappointed, but I don't know," she sighs. "I guess I wanted them to be excited, too."

I nod. "When Sara and I told our families that we were expecting Tristan, they weren't thrilled, but they came around." I tuck her under my arm. "Give 'em time."

Sutton plays with my fingers. "How'd they take it this time?"

"What do you mean?"

Her brows furrow. "What did they say when you told them about us?"

I inhale, debating whether to tell the truth, deciding the truth is best. "I don't know," I say on an exhale. "I haven't told them yet."

Sutton pulls her hand from mine, shifting away from me. Bereft of her touch, the sudden absence of her warmth startles me. It feels like I've carved a canyon between us and now I'm left standing at the edge, begging to be back in her sunlight.

She's quiet, her hands resting on her bump, staring at the sidewalk. Her shoulders rise with each breath, and it's then that I realize she's holding back tears.

"Sutton—"

She sniffles, swiping at her face before turning to me. "Why haven't you told anyone about us?"

My heart stops. Thoughts race through my head faster than I can latch onto one. Sutton watches as I fail to grasp onto something, anything to say.

She tilts her head, her eyes narrowing as I struggle to think, to breathe. Sutton's lips part as if realizing something before she nods curtly, pushing herself off the bench. "Let's go home."

How did this evening go so wrong? One minute everything's fine, and the next, we're walking together in silence back to my truck.

She doesn't protest when I guide her with my hand on her back, or when my hand grazes her ass as she steps up into the truck. But she's not leaning into my touch either.

The short drive home is silent, both of us too lost in thought to break it.

Sutton stares out of the window, absent-mindedly rubbing her stomach in slow, soothing circles. I want to reach for her hand, to let her know I'm here with her, that she's all I think about—but I don't.

I fucked up, and now I get to suffer the consequences.

She doesn't wait for my help when I park the truck in the driveway. The subtle rejection of my help, my care, stings. I watch her walk through the front door, disappearing on the other side of it.

I sit in the silent cab of the truck, listening to the ping of the cooling engine. How do I make this right? How do I fix this?

There's only one thing to do.

"Sutton," I call as soon as I step into the house, my keys clanging against the counter. I head back to our bedroom to find her attempting to take her shoes off.

"Can you help me? I think the zipper's stuck or my chubby, swollen ankles. I knew these boots were a terrible idea," she huff. She's composed herself on our silent drive, while I'm anything but.

I kneel before her, grabbing her foot and tugging the zipper free. No swollen ankles, thank god.

She moans as my thumbs slip up the arch of her foot. With both shoes off, I massage her feet, living for the hitch of her breath.

Kneeling before her, I tell her the truth, the only one I can stomach sharing for now. "I'm scared. I don't want you to think that I'm not happy to be with you, or ecstatic to be a father to our baby." My hands slide up to rest on our baby. "Please don't think I'm hiding you. I just," I suck in a breath, letting the words out on a sigh. "I need time."

Time to get my panic under control. Time to figure out what the hell I'm doing. Time to keep her safe.

"I know," she whispers, reaching out to run her hands through my hair. She does her best to hide her tears, but I notice. "This is all a lot. First, I show up at your doorstep after one night together, blow up your entire world, take over your bed and probably your sanity too," she chuckles. "You're not the only one still reeling from all this. But it doesn't mean that it doesn't sting." She strokes a thumb over my eyebrow as if it's going to release the tension.

Something inside of me deflates at the thought of ever hurting her. "I'm sorry."

She shakes her head. "Don't be. I get it."

"I don't know how to tell you how much you mean to me, Sutton. You and our baby, and Tristan, are the most important things in my life."

70

Sutton smiles softly. "I know. You might not say a lot with your words, but you show it every day."

I push up on my knees, kneeling between her spread thighs. "Have you been analyzing me?"

Her hands cup my face. "Maybe." She kisses me and everything becomes right in the world. "What're you going to do about it?" she teases.

My arm snakes around her back, pulling her closer. "Many things," I whisper, pulling her mouth to mine. She tastes like vanilla, sweet and comforting. Her lips part in a soft moan, and I deepen the kiss. Sutton grips my hair, holding me tight to her as we fall into each other.

Kissing Sutton is unlike anything I've ever experienced. Now that we've ignited this thing between us, I'm not backing down.

"Take your dress off," I order between kisses. "I want to see you." Pushing away from her, I stand, removing my clothing as I watch her strip naked. "So beautiful," I murmur, pressing kisses to her exposed collarbone.

"If you keep saying that, you're going to give me a complex." Her head falls backward, her long hair tickling against my hand at her waist as I suck a pert nipple into my mouth.

"Good." I kiss her before stepping back, the bed sinking under my weight. "Come here."

"Wait," she pauses. "What if there's something I want to do first?"

As much as I'm dying to touch her, feel her warmth around my cock, I'll wait forever for her.

I nod. "I'll be here."

She gives me a mischievous grin as she steps forward, her hands running up my thigh. My cock hardens at the glint in her eyes. Her breasts sway enticingly as she leans in, kissing my lips softly before sinking to her knees.

My chest heaves, my hands fist the comforter, and my cock aches. "Sutton."

"Let me show you how much you mean to me." She runs a hand over my hip. "You make me feel good, so let me make you feel good." Sutton doesn't break eye contact as she grasps my aching cock and wraps those perfect lips around my tip.

"Oh, fuck." Sutton moans, the vibrations stealing the breath from my lungs. She licks and sucks, her fist dragging through the wetness her mouth leaves behind, working me from root to tip. My eyes slip closed as she circles my head with her tongue.

"Uh-uh," she chastises, releasing my cock with a pop. "I want you to watch me." Slowly, I pry my eyes open to watch her as she flicks her tongue along my shaft.

"Fuck me with your mouth, Sutton. Oh, fuck, you feel so good."

She chuckles, kissing the pre-cum off my tip. "I saw how your eyes heated when I licked my ice cream. Figured you'd enjoy this."

Sutton sucks me deep and my hips jerk. "Sutton, baby, if you don't stop, I won't get to feel you before I come.

She moans, bobbing her gorgeous mouth over my cock before slowly releasing me with a pop. "Are you sure?"

My fist aches as I loosen my grip on the bedding to tilt her chin. "I've never been more sure than I am right now. I want to feel your pussy squeezing me tight." She rises as I kiss her, dragging her into my lap to straddle me.

Sutton moans as my cock glides through her wet pussy.

"Look at you, Sutton. So ready for me."

Her breathing is shallow, her breasts brushing against my chest with each inhale. "I'm always ready for you. I've never wanted someone so badly."

Sutton lifts to her knees before slowly sinking down. Her walls grip me like a vise, fluttering around me with each inch she takes.

"Look at me." My fingers tangle in her hair, gripping her head with my fist. "Baby, I want you to look at me."

Sutton and I have fucked, but this time I want more. I want to watch as she comes undone. I want to take my time, savor the taste of her lips, drown in her moans, relish the feeling of her in my arms.

Gorgeous brown eyes, hooded with lust and longing, stare into mine.

Unlike our frenzied fevered touches, we work slowly. My grip on her hair helps control our speed as she moves. Sutton rolls her hips, her hurried breaths growing more shallow.

"That's it, baby." Her walls tighten around me.

"Wells," she gasps, rolling her hips before lifting back up. "God, I love feeling you."

I laugh, my breath brushing hair away from her face. "Feeling's mutual."

My free hand grips her ass, urging her to go faster. Sweat glistens on our skin, our breath hitching. Eyes locked, we're connected beyond the point where my body stops and hers starts. At this moment, we're breathing, moving, as one.

Sutton gasps, her core tightening around me. Holding her still, I rock into her. Sutton's nails dig into my shoulders as I push her over the edge.

Eyes locked together, I watch enraptured as Sutton comes apart, her pussy pulsing around me as her body spasms.

Watching her is my undoing.

Both of us spent and panting, we sit, locked together. Hair clings to Sutton's neck and I gently wipe it away before placing kisses there.

So many unspoken words linger in the space between us. Words I can say. Words I'm holding back. But what I do know, more than anything, is that the woman in my arms, carrying my child, has a hold on my shriveled heart that's slowly coming back to life.

Chapter Ten

Sutton

"Are you sure about this?"

Wells stands shirtless in the ensuite bathroom, running his hands through his wet hair. It takes everything in me not to tilt my head, bite my lip, and beg him to come here.

He sighs, meeting my gaze in the mirror. "I'm sure."

The 'now' we're talking about is introducing me, and our surprise pregnancy, to his friends.

I understand his fears. I'm terrified about every little thing that can happen in pregnancy, but his fear stems from something more than the hypothetical—and terrifying—what ifs. I know he's holding back, and I have an idea of what it could be. But he needs time.

Nausea rolls through me. The medication I was prescribed has taken away the brunt of the non-stop sickness, but it still rears its ugly head every now and again.

My eyes slip closed as I breathe through the worst of it. I cradle my baby in my belly; the bump more pronounced in my dress.

Inhale.

Exhale.

Repeat.

Wells' hand brushes against mine, one hand drifting up to cup my clammy cheek as he kneels in front of me. Well, I assume he's kneeling since I'm sitting on the corner of our bed.

He doesn't say anything, but his presence speaks volumes. I lean into his calloused hand, focusing on the gentle circles he makes on my belly.

Wells is a complicated man. He's not straightforward. He's not open. He's a puzzle. One I'm starting to piece together.

I think it's what draws me to him.

It's that silent support, the steadfast way he comforts me without a word, that helps me through the worst of it.

"Better?" he whispers once my eyes slip back open.

I nod, smiling softly. "For now."

He rubs my belly one more time and kisses my forehead. His cologne wafts towards me and I breathe in the familiar, comforting scent. There are only a handful of smells that trigger the nausea, but not this. This I could roll around in and never get sick of.

He crosses the room to the closet, pulling out a casual shirt and dark jeans. His movements are stiff and quick.

"Are you more worried about telling Tristan or your friends?"

He stills.

Wells' situation is far more complicated than mine. There's no five-year-old running around for me to think about and take into consideration. Tristan's life is about to change. Hell, our lives are about to change, and I'm not forcing anyone to face that truth before they're ready.

He rolls his shoulders. "I'm not worried."

"Yes, you are," I chuckle. "You're wound up tighter than a jack-in-the-box and you're about to explode."

Wells finally turns to look at me, a hint of a smile on his lips. "Really? Out of all the things you could say, you came up with that?"

"You've got to admit, it's a good visual."

He laughs, picking up his shoes before sitting next to me. "You've got a way with words."

"Kelly tells me all the time." The room falls quiet as Wells ties his shoes. "You don't have to tell me if you don't want to."

"I do." Wells rests his elbows on his knees going quiet. "I guess telling everyone will make it more real."

There's more than that going on, and we both know it, but I won't push. After weeks of living together, sleeping together, there're parts of him he doesn't want to show. Bits of his past, of Sara, he won't touch. I don't know how she died, how she lived. Pictures of her are everywhere in the house, yet she's like a ghost lingering in the lines etched around his eyes.

I trace the firm muscles of his back. "Would you like me to stay here? I could see if Kelly's doing anything. You wouldn't have to tell anyone today if you don't want to."

The thought of him agreeing to my offer stings. He needs time. Space.

He shakes his head even as I say the words. Wells sits up, my hand falling down to the mattress. "Absolutely not. You're coming with me whether you want to or not." He chuckles. "There's no way I'm facing them alone. Are you kidding me? They'll eat me alive. At least with you there, they're less likely to gang up on me.

"Oh," I laugh. "So *that's* why you want me to go."

Wells chuckles, cups my face and presses a soft kiss to my lips, the warmth of them rocking me to my core. It's deep and tender, filled with all the emotions rolling within him. When he pulls back, his green eyes are full of determination. "Ready?"

TRISTAN BOUNCES FROM the car full of excitement to see his friends. Wells sat him down before we left and told him he was going to be a big brother and that a baby was growing in my belly. His reaction was hilarious. Tristan's little face scrunched up, his eyes bouncing between us before settling on my bump. Wells was more composed than I was when he asked, "How?"

My snort of hidden laughter earned me a sharp look from Wells, but I could see the twitch of a muscle as he held back his own laughter.

"Stop at the tree," Wells calls after his son, grabbing the bag of presents for Marie.

Wells has been filling me in on his friends in our nighttime chats as we lay in bed. Grant's a pediatrician with a son named Harrison and is dating a woman named Hazel. Cole's a lawyer, has two kids—Jett and Marie, who is celebrating her third birthday today—and recently hired a live-in nanny named Joanna. My brain's working overdrive so I don't forget anything and make an idiot of myself.

Tristan bounds to the sidewalk, arms swinging.

"Do you need help?" Cool fall wind blows, sending my hair and my long dress flying.

"I've got it."

One hand on my back, Wells leads me to the sidewalk and an impatient Tristan. "Can I go now?" he asks, peeking around the tree to the playground. "I see them." He points to the playground and I spot two little boys running around on the wood chips.

"Alright." The words barely leave his mouth before Tristan takes off. "Be careful!" Wells shouts, watching with eagle eyes as his son darts through the grass to the playground. Once he reaches the gate and steps through, Wells turns to me. "Ready?"

Wind blows again, my hair streaking across my face and covering my eyes. "I would be if I could see," I laugh, following slowly after him.

"Here." Wells reaches back, wrapping my hand in his. "I can't have you falling."

"Such a gentleman. Thank you." The wind picks up again, and I smooth my hand down my stomach to hold it in place.

"I hope you're prepared for questions," he sighs. The grip he has on my hand tightens minutely before relaxing. "We've been spotted."

"Are they oohing and awing?" Pink balloons bounce in the wind around a mixed group of kids and adults. The only men stand out in the crowd, and I know they're Grant and Cole.

"Oh, we've definitely made an impression."

"On a scale of one to ten, how much do you want to make a mad dash to the car?"

Wells turns, a smile wide on his face. "Zero."

"Ha," I guffaw, throwing my head back. "I bet you'll rethink that here in about two minutes."

Wells shakes his head, laughing. "Probably."

He leads us off the sidewalk, never letting go of my hand as we walk into the party. "Here we go," he says, more to himself than me.

"Hey, Wells." A pretty woman with gorgeous auburn curls takes Marie's present. She smiles warmly at me, offering her hand. "I'm Hazel. Nice to meet you..."

"Sutton. I've heard a lot about you."

She smiles even wider. "Really?" Hazel raises an eyebrow at Wells. "I'm surprised he knows how to talk." I can't help it. I laugh. "So he didn't kidnap you," she teases. "Good to know."

A smothered chuckle has me turning to look at Wells' friends. "Sutton, this is Grant and Cole." I shake their hands. "And yes, she's heard about you."

Both men are impressive and attractive. Almost as attractive as Wells, but I'm biased. Grant drapes his arm around Hazel, pulling her close.

"We're glad you're here," Cole says. "Thanks for coming." He smiles at me before looking over his shoulder, his eyes softening.

"I'm happy to be party crashing." Kids laugh and play on the playground while parents sit and supervise. A blonde woman works to set up food, a little girl with a princess tiara trailing after her. "Is there anything I can help with?"

I know Wells doesn't want me to leave his side and act like a buffer, but I can see his friends are itching to grill him about me. Honestly, the thought of him squirming in his boots makes me laugh.

"Cole?" The blonde woman walks over, the little girl on her hip crying. "I think someone's ready to eat." She looks at me. "Hi, I'm Joanna."

I smile and wave as the little girl squeals and wiggles in her arms. I don't miss the way Cole's gaze rakes up and down her body or the heat behind his eyes when he looks at his nanny. Interesting.

Grant pulls Wells and Cole to the side while I trail after Hazel and Joanna.

Tristan runs up with two other boys, grabbing drinks from a cooler and chugging them down before dashing off. Hazel calls after them, letting them know it's almost time to eat before turning to me. "I'm dying to know how you and Wells met."

Chapter Eleven

Wells

The Macy's Thanksgiving Parade blares from the television. Tristan's bouncing on his toes watching the spectacle with wide, joyful eyes. It's not my favorite, but Sara loved it and I wanted him to share something with her.

Acorns, leaves and pumpkins decorate the entire house. Tristan and I came home the first Sunday of November after hanging out at Cole's house to find it transformed. Sutton looked so happy, her cheeks a rosy pink from exertion as Kelly balanced on a chair hanging garland across the entrance to the hall.

She's been with her family all week. With her classes pausing, belly growing, and the holiday, it made sense for her to travel while she can.

God, I miss her.

I know she's with her family, and perfectly safe, but it has me on edge. She's hours away. If something goes wrong, there's no way for me to get there quickly.

Both mom and baby are healthy, despite Sutton's extreme morning sickness. No matter how many times I remind myself, my mind still whirrs. Is she eating enough? Did she remember to take her medication? Is she having a hard time sleeping too? Because without her in my arms, sleep has become non-existent.

My eyes flick to the kitchen, where the black and tan 3-D ultrasound hangs proudly on the fridge. Chubby cheeks, pouty lips, and clasped hands fill the image. The name Baby Boyd sits in the upper right corner of the picture, the gender left blank. It's been the constant reminder throughout the week they're both healthy, and I breathe easier.

"Look at Bluey, Dad!" Tristan's bright face turns to me before going back to the screen. Sure enough, Bluey floats in the air above the New York crowds.

"I see it." My son goes wild at seeing his favorite characters as they float above the street. But it doesn't take long for Tristan to let out a wet cough. My small son's shoulders shake as he struggles to loosen up the gunk in his chest. Grant said it was a cold and that they're going around this time of year, but I can't help but freeze.

Born premature, Tristan gets sicker than most kids. He's behind in so many ways; from his stunted growth to his fragile immune system. Thankfully, he's mostly overcome the two months spent in the NICU, but the effects still linger in more ways than one.

"I think it's time for you medicine," I say, setting my coffee down on the side table.

Tristan slumps. "But I don't want to take them," he whines.

"Too bad. C'mon." I shake the bottle, the medicine sloshing inside as Tristan drags his feet. "Want milk or juice?" The small measuring cup fills with the grape flavor cough syrup.

"Ugh," he groans, his shoulders drooping as he lets his arms hang.

"Pick one or you get none." I learned early on that if he has something to take afterwards, he's more willing to agree. Sutton thinks it's hilarious that I offer my kid a chaser, but it works.

"Can I get a pop? Sutton gets to have some when my brother makes her sick."

"We don't know if it's a boy. You could have a sister."

He scrunches his face. "I don't want a sister."

"Well, we'll find out in about three months." The fridge clicks open. The two liter of clear pop sits on the top shelf. It might be early, but I'll let it slide. "Here." I hand him the cup of medicine to take while I fill a juice cup.

He makes a face as he swallows, making me laugh before he reaches for the cup I hold out. "That stuff's nasty."

"Yeah, I know." I run my fingers through his blonde hair a few shades darker than his mothers.

It's been over five years since Sara died, almost six in a month. Time passes so slowly, yet faster than lightning.

We spend the rest of the morning watching the parade before football starts. Later this evening, we'll head to my parent's house on the eastside of Indianapolis to spend the holiday with family, even though the one person I can't stop thinking about is hundreds of miles away.

As if she can sense my thoughts, Sutton's face lights up my screen. She's smiling at the camera, her cheeks a dusty rose, hair piled on top of her head as she lays in bed. I'm not sure when she took it, but it's my favorite.

"Are you surviving?" I say into the phone as I close the door to our bedroom.

Sutton chuckles. "Barely. Mom's been a hovering mess, which reminds me of someone, but I can't put my finger on who..."

"Ha-ha. At least someone's taking care of you." Although she doesn't like it, it does settle some of the worry in my chest.

"Eh. She's not you." I picture the way the corner of her mouth tilts up when she teases. "Dad's better, though. I think he's more excited than mom now. Keeps saying he wants to, quote, 'take his grandson to his first Cardinals Game.'"

Sutton's dad, Chris, isn't my biggest fan. From what Sutton has told me, his reaction to her pregnancy was anything but happy. I'm glad to hear he's coming around, though. Having him be excited about his grandchild, even if it's forcing the Cardinals on our child, is a welcomed change.

I scoff. "Over my dead body."

"Ha," she chortles. "I told him you're a Cubs fan. That may be why he keeps saying it. Dad may have already gotten a Cardinals onesie."

I shake my head, but that doesn't keep the smile off my face. "Putting poor team choice aside, how's everything else going?" She knows what question I'm really asking.

She sighs. "Wells."

The mattress gives under my weight with a creak. "Tell me you're okay. Please." I run a hand down my face. A part of me won't calm down until I hear her say it. I'll spend the rest of my day with a ball of worry in my stomach if she doesn't.

We've never talked about it. Sutton's observant, often noticing things without me needing to say them. This is one of those things. I'll tell her my full story one day, but right now, I need to know she's okay.

"Wells, we're okay. Baby is moving all the time. Honestly, they're bouncing all over my bladder. I have to pee every ten minutes, which is highly annoying. We're about to eat Thanksgiving lunch, so I'm eating, not to mention, Grams made her coffee cake for breakfast, so I've had way too much of that." She chuckles. "I'm fine."

Relief floods through me. "Good," I say with an exhale.

"There is one thing, though. It's new, so I'm not all that used to it yet. It could be serious."

My scalp prickles. "Yeah?"

"I miss you. And Tristan. How's he doing with his cold?"

Warmth grows in my chest at her words. "Don't do that to me," I warn, letting out a relieved sigh. She laughs, helping to soothe the ball of anxiety that sprang into my chest at her words. "Tristan's stubborn, like someone else I know." Sutton snickers. "The cough is still bad, but I got him to take his medicine. He's been watching the parade all morning."

"Did he get to see Chase?"

"Oh, he saw all the Paw Patrol characters." He cheered and ran circles around the living room when he saw them. "I sent you the video."

Sutton gasps. "You did? I haven't checked my phone. With everyone showing up at the house, it's been crazy." On cue, peels of laughter ring out in the background, growing louder as more people talk over each other.

"It sounds like you've got to go."

"It does." She sounds as reluctant as I feel.

I close my eyes, picturing her beautiful face. "I miss you, Sutton. I can't wait until you're home and in my arms. Please take care of yourself. Of both of you."

"We'll be home soon, Wells. I'll call you later when I can."

"I lo—," I clear my throat, those three words I've been feeling almost leaving my lips. "I'll uh, let you go."

Sutton's quiet on the other end. People laugh in the distance as we sit in silence.

We both know what I was going to say. There's no denying it.

"Bye, Wells."

IT'S BEEN A LONG DAY. Stomachs full of turkey and stuffed with pie, Tristan and I finally make it home. Sutton has texted me once since our phone call, but I know she's busy, safe at her family's house in Missouri. I'll see her this weekend.

As I get Tristan ready for bed and tuck him in, Sutton's all I can think about. The only thing on my mind as I shower and slip into our bed.

It's been hard sleeping without her. I never thought I'd get used to sharing a bed with anyone after Sara, but here I am. Without Sutton's warm, lush body pressing against mine, I'm left cold and alone.

Sleep finally lingers at the edges, slowly tugging me under inch by inch. I'm in the in-between, suspended in that space between reality and dreams. The featherlight stroke of imaginary fingers tingle at my temples. Warm lips pressing against my cheek.

Even at the cusp of sleep, she's here. The feeling of her phantom touch is enough to make me moan.

Hot breath tickles my neck. "Are you awake now?" Sutton's sweet and floral shampoo fills my nose. It's the same smell that haunted me all those months ago.

"No," I mumble, fighting against the surge to the surface of consciousness.

A breathy laugh tickles my ear. "You sure? You're saying I drove all this way and you're not even awake? It took longer than expected, too, because blob was bouncing on my bladder every fifteen minutes."

My eyes snap open. Not a dream. It's not my subconscious creating shadows in a poor replica of the real thing. "Sutton?" I blink, willing my vision to adjust to the darkness.

She's perched on the edge of our bed, one arm bracing at my side. Her hair is a mess of frizzy waves, as if she's just run her fingers through it. Or held them back. "There he is." A warm smile crosses her lips. "Did you have a nice dream?"

I sit up so fast; she gasps right as I cup her face and kiss her. Surrounded by her smell, the warmth of her skin, the comfort of her being in my arms is everything I've longed for all week.

Sutton clings to me as we lose ourselves to the kiss. It's impossible to tell where I end and she begins. We're a mess of searching limbs and seeking lips. She gasps as I push her onto her back and settle between her spread thighs. "How are you here?"

"Drove. Left after we ate." She gasps as I slip my hand under her sweater, brushing my thumb over her peaked nipple. "I missed you."

"Did you?" I smile against her lips.

She laughs. "Hard to believe. I know. Ah." I pinch her nipple, stealing the breath from her lungs, loving the sounds of her pleasure. "I missed you, too."

"Wells," she pants, her fingers sliding below the waistband of my shorts. Now I'm the one groaning as she wraps her hand around my hard cock. "I thought of you the whole drive here. Thought I would die if I didn't see you. Didn't get to put my hands on you." She works my cock, dragging moans from my lips.

I pull myself away from her and off the bed, leaving her gaping at me. Hungry eyes watch as I rid myself of my shorts before holding my hand out to her. She takes it, letting me drag her off the bed. I touch and kiss every inch of her as I methodically remove her clothing.

"You think I didn't want you in my arms? Didn't think about you for every second we were apart? Fuck Sutton, I was losing my goddamn mind without you." Her bra falls away, her gorgeous breasts bouncing with each ragged breath. "You're so beautiful, you know that? A fucking angel." Fingers trail down between the valley of her breasts, stopping to rest against the bump of her belly.

She presses a palm to my pounding heart. Tears brim in her eyes as her lips part. "I felt it too."

We both know the words I'm not saying. The words I can't bring to utter past my lips. Not yet.

My hand drifts lower, cupping her pussy. She's so wet, I groan. Sutton's eyes slip closed as my fingers circle her clit. "Wells," she breathes, leaning into me.

"I need to feel you, baby." I sink two fingers into her wet heat, cursing as she squeezes around me. "Are you ready for me, baby?"

Her hips rock into my hand as I tease her pussy. "Yes."

I pull her in for a messy kiss, her whimper of pleasure drowning out in my throat. "Get on the bed. Let me see that ass."

"God, I missed that bossiness." She smiles at me over her shoulder as she gets situated on the bed. I snatch a pillow and place it under her hips.

With her growing belly, we've had to get creative.

Velvet smooth skin glides beneath my palm, running down her spine. She shivers in anticipation as I cup her ass. "You're perfect."

"Wells, please." Sutton wiggles her ass, looking back at me with impatience.

"God, I love when you beg." I grip my cock, lining it up with her entrance, and she groans. Slowly, I sink into her, moaning her name. "I missed you."

"Please. Don't stop."

Each thrust is slow. Deliberate. I savor every squeeze of her cunt, every gasp and moan. Her hands grip the sheets as mine squeeze her hips. Words of praise and adoration leave my lips.

She's mine.

To love.

Praise.

Cherish.

Care for.

Desire.

She's the person I never knew I needed. Sutton streaked across my dark sky like a blazing comet, casting her warm glow upon everything she touches."I need you," I confess, sinking deep.

"Oh, god, Wells." Sutton's beautiful, with sweat glistening along her spine, her dark hair tossed over one shoulder, her brown eyes never leaving mine. "Faster. Please, Wells. Let me feel you. Ah, I'm close."

I smirk as her pussy clenches around me. "Hold on, baby. I've got you." Hooking an arm around her hip, I find her clit, circling it with a delicate touch. She mewls, her eyes slipping closed as she buries her face in the sheets. "That's it, baby."

Within moments, Sutton's writhing against me, pushing back with each thrust as her climax rolls through her.

Her climax triggers mine, both of us losing ourselves in the other.

Calm and sated, I hold her in my arms, tracing the lines of her face, the angle of her neck, the curve of her breasts, the circle of her belly. "Was being home so bad?" I squeeze her ass. "I can't say I'm mad you came back."

"Oh, it wasn't bad," she says with a laugh. Her hand strokes along my jaw. "Not as good as this, though. Nothing could top this."

I hum, leaning in to kiss her lips. "Just how I like it." Her eyes soften. Something is bothering her. It's in the way her eyes trail across my face, the sudden inhale through her nose, the tension set across those luscious lips. "What?"

Sutton sighs, dropping her hand to tuck it underneath her chin. It feels as if I've stepped out into a blizzard, all warmth leaving my body with the loss of her touch. "Are you sure about this, Wells?"

Confusion has me jolting back. "Sure about what?"

"Everything. Me, the baby—"

"Sutton."

She silences me with a touch to my lips. "I showed up on your front porch and literally flipped your life upside down. I've taken over your home, your sense of peace. Don't think I don't notice the worry, the panic I sometimes see in your eyes."

Her words slice right through my heart. "You, Tristan, and our baby mean everything to me. Don't," I press a finger against her puckering lips. "Don't try to reason this away. I don't want a world without you in it."

I've had my world ripped away from me once before. Lived without the person filling my chest with breath. But I know now that I can't survive that again.

Sutton goes quiet, tears silently brimming in her eyes. Sucking in a steadying breath, she says the words that break me. "But you're still holding back."

Chapter Twelve

Sutton

"You're in the home stretch, Sutton." Plastic gloves snap as Doctor Diana stands, tossing the discarded gloves into the trash. "Baby looks healthy. All your testing came back normal: blood, urine, glucose. How's the morning sickness?"

Wells grabs my hand, helping me sit up. Normal things that used to be easy are near impossible with the basketball in my stomach. Getting dressed has me winded, and putting shoes on is impossible without him.

Wells has been quiet the last few weeks. More quiet than normal, I should say. I blame myself for that.

If I would've just kept my big mouth shut, there wouldn't be this awkwardness between us. It feels like when I first moved in with him. I can feel his eyes on me, sense something brewing within him, but he won't tell me. All because I put my enormous foot in my mouth.

It's easy to tell that Wells is struggling with something. The man might not say much, but everything about him is loud. The way his face goes pale, the thin line of his mouth, the slight shake of the head. He's dealing with something, struggling with something, and he won't talk to me about it.

Hell, I'm studying to be a therapist, and I can't get him to open up to me. I'm not blind. I've always known there was something eating away at him, but I thought waiting until he was ready was the right way to go. But I had to open my stupid mouth and now he's shut down.

"Um, it depends. Some days are better than others. But my nurse here makes sure I'm eating and drinking enough." Wells smiles at me, but it doesn't quite reach his eyes.

Doctor Diana nods before asking more questions about how I'm feeling, and more probing questions about my pregnancy. Wells sits silent through it all, soaking up every answer. He draws comforting circles along my back, giving me silent support like he always does.

The wheels of the office stool squeak as she faces me. "We'll start seeing you bi-weekly to monitor you and baby."

I nod, dragging a hand down my belly. It's been both the longest and shortest thirty weeks of my life. And now, it's all happening so fast.

Dressed and with an appointment card in hand because of my pregnancy brain, Wells walks us out to his truck. His touch never leaves me as he helps me step up into the cab. "Can we make a stop before we head home? There's something I'd like to show you."

"Sure."

SNOW CLINGS TO THE grass in a thin film as Wells guides me down the sidewalks at Liberty College. I know them well, having spent my fair share of time trudging across campus for early morning lectures or late night outings. I'm not sure why he's brought us here in the middle of January, but I know I'll find out soon enough.

We're nearing the edge of campus, past the buildings and dorms, and I know exactly where we're headed. "You could've said we're going to Lover's Pond. Would've saved me from wondering what we're doing here."

Wells chuckles. "What? And ruin the suspense?"

Lover's pond is exactly what it sounds like. The official name is after some hoity-toity donor or something, but we all know it as Lover's Pond. It's the go-to spot on campus. During the summer, there's a walking trail and people picnicking. In the winter, like now, when the water is frosted over and there's nothing to stop the harsh winds, it's deserted.

Wells leads me to a bench and I rub my hands together to keep them warm. I feel trapped in my giant puffer coat, scarf, and gloves, but the wind seems to cut through all the layers. "Shit, it's cold."

"Sorry." He sits close, our thighs touching as he wraps an arm around my shoulder and holds me close. "I should've come up with somewhere inside, but this is the place that reminds me the most of her."

Sara.

He doesn't notice my hand on his thigh offering whatever comfort I can. He's busy caught up in memories. I let him sit with them for as long as he needs. Wells stares out across the pond before sucking in a deep breath. "I know you want me to let you in, and God Sutton, I want that."

"If you're not ready—"

"That's the thing. I'll never be ready. But I want you to know every part of me, Sutton."

Wind stings my eyes as I fight back tears. "Okay."

Tension sits underneath his skin. He breathes deeply, those green eyes slipping closed as if to steady himself. If we have to sit in the cold for the rest of the day, then I'll do it. I might have to take a bathroom break here and there, but I won't leave until he's ready. Won't push him to share whatever it is he's battling with.

Minutes pass as the wind blows over the frozen pond. Bare branches creak, the wind whistling through them. It's utterly quiet.

Wells sighs, reaching down to hold my hand resting on his thigh. "This is where I met Sara. It was freshman year. Classes hadn't even started. It was the block party and there were crowds of people."

I nod, even though he's not looking at me. The week leading up to classes at Liberty, there's all sorts of mixer events to help people get to know one another. Food vendors, live music, inflatable games, the works.

"I saw her and couldn't look away. She was...*everything*." He sniffles. "We were married young. God, looking back, we were just babies ourselves."

He's not sharing anything I didn't already know. There are many conversations we've shared in the dark of our room at night before sleep as we cuddle together. They were young and in love. Younger than I am now.

"It wasn't long before we found out she was pregnant." Tears are falling down his cheeks. He doesn't bother wiping them away. "She was so excited. We both were."

"She found a tiny house for rent and started decorating the baby room. I was busy working, getting the business up and running, so I wasn't able to make her doctor's appointments. She came back telling me that everything was fine."

Wells loosens his hold before running his gloved palm over my stomach. Over our baby.

"She didn't get sick, but as she got farther along, she started to swell. Feet, hands, ankles." He chuckles at a memory. "Sara was in her last trimester, absolutely glowing. She complained about small stuff: headaches, nausea, fatigue. Her doctor told her it was normal and nothing to worry about."

Dread fills my chest. I know what he's going to say before he speaks the words.

His voice breaks. "She was home alone."

I suck in a breath, a lone tear trailing down my cheek.

"It was late when I got home from work." He swallows hard before continuing. "They, uh, rushed her to the hospital, but it was too late. Too much damage. They were lucky to even get Tristan out before it was too late."

My heart breaks, rips in two for the man I love. There are no words I could say, nothing I can do, except listen and be here for him as he shares his story.

Red-rimmed eyes meet mine. "That's why I'm so fucking scared, Sutton. Seeing you the night we met, I felt my heart beat again for the first time in years. There was no one else for me. I saw no one else, heard no one else." Wells grips my face, his thumb wiping away my tears. "I love you so much that I won't survive if I lose you."

"Wells..." He shakes his head, silencing me.

"When I found you, all alone on the floor of your bathroom, I'd never been so terrified. I couldn't let anything happen to you. To our baby. That's what I've been holding back. I'm so fucking scared that you'll..." His eyes shut, trying to hold back the tears that are already falling.

My fingers freeze, but I don't care. Tugging off my gloves, I cup his face, letting him feel my soothing touch. He's been carrying so much this whole time. I knew he was scared. I knew he had a past, but I didn't know the full extent of his trauma.

Wells sucks in a breath, slowly letting it out. His green eyes are glassy with unshed tears, but the ghosts within them are gone. For so long he's been suffering, holding his pain, his terror inside. Shouldering the weight of it alone. "I blamed myself for Sara's death. I didn't do enough. When you showed up on my porch, I knew I couldn't make the same mistakes again." He leans down, kissing me softly.

"Wells, you've been the most amazing partner. I don't think I could've found anyone better if I tried." He huffs a laugh, smiling down at me. "I love you, you know."

Wells nods. "I love you. So much. More than I thought I could love another person."

We sit, looking out over the frozen lake. I know what he's seeing as he stares at the place where they met. He's seeing the woman he loved. The mother of his son. Someone he lost that shattered his world.

He was so scared. Holding it all in, bottling it up. My heart breaks for him. Silent tears stream down my cheeks. He's lost so much and he's still here, trying to make up for what he thinks he did wrong.

"Thank you. For sharing with me." Stubble brushes along my thumb as I rub his jaw, tilting his face to kiss him.

Wells holds me close to his chest, wrapping me in his warmth. "Can I take you home?"

"Always."

WELLS HOLDS MY HAND, not complaining when I lead him down the hallway, through our shared bedroom, and into the bathroom. His hands rest on my hips as I unzip his coat, pull his shirt over his head, unbuckle his belt. "Shower with me?"

A rough hand cups my jaw. Wells kisses me slowly and I savor the weight of his hand on my hip. He pulls away all too soon, brushing his thumb along my chin as he nods.

Steam rises as the water quickly warms. I shiver, wrapping my arms around myself before Wells pulls me against him, the hot water trailing down my skin. For a moment, we stand in an embrace as the water warms us. Wells sighs as I kiss his chest over his heart. "Penny for your thoughts?"

My laugh echos. Our first doctor's appointment. The first time we spent alone after our night together. "I was thinking how lucky I am to have you."

"I think you've got it backwards," he says, turning us and letting the water wet my hair. Strong fingers massage my scalp and my eyes slip closed. "It never ceases to amaze me that you're here. That I get to come home to you and my son. I used to dread it, you know. Coming home was a reminder of the past, but now," he sighs, "it's filled with hope. I can't wait to see our child grow up. To see Tristan have a sibling. To love you."

This time, when our lips touch, it's no longer slow. Familiar heat sparks at the taste of his lips, the drag of his tongue. All of the emotion from the last several hours is poured into this kiss. Love, anxiety, hope. It's there in every reverent touch, every strangled moan.

Wells kisses my neck, my shoulder, and down to my breasts. My hands slick through his wet hair as he gently sucks on my nipple, and I hiss. "Sensitive?" he asks.

"Very." The further into pregnancy I've gotten, the more my body has changed. My breasts are fuller and more sensitive than I could've imagined.

He kisses my sternum. "Turn around, baby." I do as I'm told. Wells brushes my wet hair over a shoulder. Hot lips travel down my spine, his hand gliding over my pregnant belly and cupping my pussy. "I love you so much, Sutton. You came in and breathed life back into me."

Fingers slip through my folds before sinking into my center. My hands flex against the cold tiles as he pumps his fingers into me. Wells' hard cock presses into my ass, and I clench around his fingers. He slips his fingers from my pussy, dragging them up to circle my clit. I moan, my hips pressing against his cock in welcome.

Wells aligns himself with my aching core before slowly sinking in. His fist clenched tight around my hip, keeping me still. Seated deep within me, Wells drags my back against his chest, his arms wrapping around me and holding me upright. With every languid thrust, Wells releases everything he's held on to. I feel his pain, his sorrow, his joy with each push of his hips. Words of praise and adoration float around me.

"I love you," I whisper over and over as he makes love to me. And I do. I see every part of this man: his love, his devotion, his trauma, and I love it all. He says that I'm the one that brought him back to life, but he's the one that's given me a life I never dreamed of. Love I never dared to think about.

Pleasure spirals through me, my inner muscles clenching around him as I come. Strong arms hold me up when my legs threaten to give out, but not for one second would he let me fall.

Clutched against his chest, Wells moans my name as he climaxes.

On steady feet, Wells pulls out of me. The loss of him is jarring, but he pulls me close, kissing me. "Will you stay?"

I cup his jaw, meeting his gaze. He's not talking about right now, he's talking about our future. Our forever. "I'm not going anywhere. I promise."

Chapter Thirteen

Sutton

"Whoa. Hey, big mama. Looks like you've been throwing down some fertilizer on little blob." Kelly greets my belly first, planting her hands on both sides of my giant belly and leaning in close. "You better stay in there as long as you can. I can't have my new best friend make an early appearance."

"I am right here, you know."

Kelly murmurs sweet nothings to my belly, completely ignoring me. She gasps, pressing her palm to my right side. Wide-eyed, Kelly looks up at me, an astonished grin slipping across her face. "Did blob just move?"

"Technically, they kicked." I wince as blob pushes into my ribs. "It's getting to be a tight squeeze in there." So tight that my hips ache, my lower back is on fire, and it feels like blob is pushing on my vagina, which has to be one of the most uncomfortable things I've ever felt. So, yeah. There's no space left for them to go.

"God, I can't wait to see their little face." Kelly bends down, whispering to my belly, "Only three more weeks blob and then you'll have a name. But I think blob is gonna stick around for a while."

"No, it's not," Wells mutters as he and Cole move tables in the small cafe.

Kelly scoffs. "Good thing you can't tell me what to do, baby daddy." She straightens. "Baby is now forever going to be called blob just to spite him. It's decided."

I roll my eyes. "Aren't you supposed to be helping with all this?" I gesture around the room at all the decorations.

After meeting them at the park, Hazel and Joanna have become fast friends of mine. When Kelly mentioned wanting to throw me a baby shower, Hazel and Joanna threw their support behind it. The three of them planned this entire thing. The only thing I have to do is show up.

"I am," she says with a smile. "I'm playing hostess and making sure the very heavily pregnant person of honor makes it to their very comfortable seat." She loops her arm around mine and helps me waddle towards the blue suede chair set up in front of the bay window. Once she makes sure I'm all situated, she flits off, her chest length braid flopping over her shoulder.

I can't believe we're here. These thirty-seven weeks have simultaneously been the longest and shortest weeks of my life. It's almost hard to believe how much has happened since finding out about blob all those months ago.

My stomach tightens uncomfortably. I adjust in my chair and run a comforting hand down my stomach. Wells notices, of course. He raises a concerned eyebrow and I wave him off, giving him a tight smile. Worry still etches the lines on his face, but he nods, getting back to being bossed around by Kelly, Hazel, and Joanna.

It doesn't take long for people to show up. College friends, co-workers, and family mingle together in the small cafe. Wells' parents made the trip into town and help wrangle Jett, Harrison, Marie, and Tristan as they play in the corner. They're full of kind smiles and warm hugs. My baby will be well loved. My parents are coming closer to my due date, so they won't be here for several weeks. They made sure to shower me with all sorts of baby items when they came down for Christmas.

The muscles of my back tighten, looping around to my sides. Blob flips, pushing against me, adding to the uncomfortableness. It's fine, though. Nothing I can't handle.

DESIRED BY THE SINGLE DAD

My college friends and I stand in a circle, chatting about what they're up to. The whole time I work on schooling my features. The skirt of my dress sways as I fight against the cramps in my belly.

"Classes are good," I smile to keep myself from wincing. "Most of my work is online, and thanks to my job, I'm able to get in some clinical hours. Thankfully, I've been able to work ahead, so I won't get behind once the baby gets here."

"Wow, that's impressive. Pretty sure I would've flunked out if it were me." Bowie laughs at herself before sipping her punch. "Hell, I can barely keep up with work and my crazy ass family."

Bowie was in nursing courses with Kelly. The two of them spent hours filling our tiny apartment with giant text books and flashcards studying for their classes.

When it's time to open gifts, it's harder to control my face. Sweat beads at the back of my neck, thankfully hidden by my hair. Wells stands behind me, one hand on my shoulder as Hazel and Joanna pass me the gifts. I smile, showing off each gift and reading the cards before passing them off to Kelly.

"Hey, babe, is everything alright?" she whispers as I hand off a basket full of wipes and diapers. "You look a little pale."

I nod, putting on a brave face. "I'm all good." Smile through it. It's no big deal. It doesn't hurt that much.

Kelly furrows her brow. "Does she look pale to you?" she asks Wells.

Well, shit. Here we go. This nice party that people put so much effort into is going to end abruptly, I can tell.

Wells crouches in front of me, his hand slipping behind my head. I know he feels the sweat on my neck, but he doesn't say anything. The man I love simply studies my face. Under his green gaze, I know he can see everything I've been working to hide.

"How long?" A soothing hand runs up and down my thigh.

I smile softly, playing dumb. "How long, what?"

"Baby, how long have you been having contractions?" Locked in those loving eyes, the rest of the room fades into the background. There are no longer friends and family watching our interaction. There's no kids laughing in the corner or the sound of crashing blocks.

It's just me and him.

"Since we got here."

He nods. "How long in between?"

I shrug right as another wave hits. This time it encompasses my entire torso, wrapping around me and squeezing, knocking the air from my lungs. There's no hiding it this time.

"Breathe, baby. That's it." Wells' calm voice gives me something to focus on.

Next to me, Kelly swears. "How did I know this was going to happen?" Cool fingers wrap around my wrist as she takes my pulse.

I focus on my breathing, inhaling and exhaling with Wells until the worst of it passes. I'm thankful he's come to every appointment and child birthing class, because every ounce of information has left my brain.

Hushed voices fall around us, and when I open my eyes, Grant's nodding at something Wells says before patting him on the shoulder. Cole stands back, his arms crossed watching his friend with worry.

"Okay, baby. We're going to the hospital."

"What? Why? It's fine, I can—"

"We're going, Sutton." His tone leaves no room for argument. "Please. I can't..." he trails off, his Adam's apple bobbing.

Within moments, Kelly makes an announcement as Wells leads me through the cafe. Tristan runs up, his little face so cute and confused. "Where are you going?"

Wells kneels in front of him. "Sutton and I are going to the hospital. Your little brother or sister is coming."

Tristan looks up at me. "Are you coming back?"

It's like an arrow to the heart. A broken sob sneaks out of Wells, his eyes glazing over with tears as he looks back at me. "Of course," I tell them both. "Before you know it, we'll be introducing you to your baby sibling."

Tristan nods before leaning towards my belly and planting a sweet kiss. I can't hear what he says, but Wells smiles, pulling his son in for a hug and kissing him firmly on the forehead before sending him to his grandparents.

We have to stop in the parking lot as another contraction hits. The palm of Wells' hand rubs firm circles on my hips, talking me through the pain before gently lifting me into his truck.

Love mixed with worry etches his face as he looks at me. "Ready to have our baby?"

Chapter Fourteen

Wells

It's been twenty-four hours. A whole fucking day of Sutton contorting her face in pain. Of Sutton refusing any type of pain medication.

Twenty-four hours of my heart ripping out of my chest.

Every second that I sit here, holding Sutton's hand, rubbing her back, brushing her hair out of her face, is agony. Too much. It's all too much and I'm slowly starting to break.

Doctor Diana has been in several times, coming in to talk with our nurse, Kendra, about how Sutton's progressing. Last night, she almost sent us home making my chest swell with panic at the thought. But luckily, Sutton had dilated enough that it was clear we would be staying overnight.

Sutton hasn't slept. Hasn't eaten. She's so tired, and if I could take all her pain away, I would. Sweat coats her neck, slicks down the hair at her nape. She turns on her side, silently forging through the pain. I don't know how she does it.

Kelly stops by, sneaking into labor and delivery for a few minutes on her shift. She held a cool cloth to Sutton's brow and neck before kissing her cheek. She gave me a very stern warning of calling her the second anything changes. If there's one thing I know about Kelly, it's that she will do anything for people she cares about. That and any possible threat she sends my way is credible.

Sutton's parents have made their way into town, coming by periodically to check on their daughter. They both wrapped me in warm hugs when they first got here, her dad patting me on the back before going to see his little girl. They had to leave once visiting hours ended, but I promised I would keep them updated on how Sutton's doing. Since visiting at Christmas, her parents have warmed to the idea of me, and I'm glad for Sutton's sake.

Between contractions, Sutton's able to relax. She studies my face as I sit next to her, one hand clasping hers while the other runs up and down her back. A clammy palm cups my cheek, her thumb running over the crease of my brow. "You need to sleep."

I shake my head, turning it to kiss her palm. "Not while you're in pain."

She laughs half-heartedly. "Hate to break it to you, but that's what childbirth is. There's no need for the two of us to be exhausted when the baby comes. Lay down, close your eyes, and dream of dancing babies."

I laugh. "Dancing babies?"

"I was trying to think of something comforting."

"You could've said laying at home with our baby on my chest, Tristan sleeping on one side and you on the other. Because that's what I want right now."

"But would it have made you laugh?"

I shake my head. "Probably not."

We sit like that, her thumb brushing across my cheek, looking at each other with such hope that my dream becomes a reality.

Sutton stiffens against me, her breathing becoming more labored. Our baby's heartbeat whooshes from the monitor strapped around her stomach as her contraction rolls through her.

There's a soft knock on the door before Kendra pokes her head in. "How's everything going? Are we having another contraction?"

I nod as Sutton rocks back and forth on her side. "She's getting through it." I might not be, but she's stronger than I am.

Sutton slumps against the mattress, completely exhausted. Kendra grips the handles of the bed, her voice soft. "How ya feelin', Momma?"

Sutton lets out a huff. "Oh, I think I've been better."

"I'd say." Kendra smiles. "You've been at this a long time. Is it okay if I check you? Feel free to tell me to get the hell away if you want."

Sutton shifts on the mattress. "No, I wanna know where we're at." Her tired eyes drift to me. "I'm not sure how much longer I can do this for."

She's so exhausted. If I could do this for her, I would in a heartbeat. Seeing her in any sort of pain or discomfort has always eaten away at me.

Kendra puts on a glove, and I stand, making room for her. The room falls quiet as Kendra focuses on measuring Sutton's cervix. She sighs, shaking her head. "Still at eight."

"Only eight?" Sutton groans. "I've been at eight for hours." Doctor Diana started some sort of drip to help her labor along. After all this time, nothing has seemed to help.

"I know," Kendra says sympathetically. "Sometimes it takes longer than we want. But you know you can always change your mind if you want an epidural. The last thing we want is for you to be too tired to push."

Sutton's eyebrows slant across her face in worry. "What do you think?"

Me? I want her to be out of pain and able to rest. But I won't make that decision for her. "It's up to you, baby."

A delicate hand swipes across her brow before resting on the top of her head. "I don't think I can do this." Tears well in her eyes as she breaks..

Kendra excuses herself, slipping quietly out of the room, but not before letting me know to page her if we need her.

I crawl into bed behind Sutton, wrapping my arms around her as she cries. She covers her face as the tears fall. She's exhausted, and in pain, and it doesn't look like the end is in sight. All I can do is hold her, comfort her, whisper soft words of praise of how well she's doing, how strong she is, that she can do this. We can do this.

Another contraction hits. This close to her, I can feel her muscles tense as her body works to prepare for delivery. A heartbreaking cry slips through her lips as it ratchets up in intensity. Once over, she sags against me, voice broken. "I think I need an epidural."

Within half an hour, the anesthesiologist knocks on the door, wheeling in his kit.

Sutton's head rests on my chest as she leans over the edge of the bed. The doctor talks her through the procedure, occasionally instructing her to curve her spine more. She hisses when the needle punctures her skin, her hands gripping tight to my shirt as the doctor does his job.

Within twenty minutes, Sutton's asleep.

We both sleep for hours. I occasionally wake as more nurses come in, checking Sutton's vitals and monitoring the baby's heart rate. When they start coming in more frequently, I sit up.

"Is everything okay?" Nurse Kendra's shift ended shortly after Sutton's epidural, promising to check on us when she gets back. Nurse Wendi gives me a tight smile.

"When you're in labor this long, it can start to wear on both mom and baby." She looks down at Sutton, her mouth slightly open in sleep. "We want to make sure everyone continues to stay healthy."

Panic swirls through me. "Are they okay?"

Wendi smiles. She's an older lady with streaks of gray in her short ponytail. "Doctor Arnold should be here soon to go over some things with you."

I know she's trying to be comforting to keep me calm, but I'm anything but calm right now. I haven't been fucking calm in nine months.

Sutton stirs, her lashes fluttering before those brown eyes settle on me. She yawns, pulling her arms over her head as she stretches. "I needed that. How long did I sleep?"

My sneakers squeak as I pace beside her bed. "Around five hours."

"Wow. I should've gotten this epidural yesterday." She holds out her hand. "Come here." I take it, swiping my free hand through my tousled hair. "You're going to pull all your hair out if you keep doing that." She presses a kiss on the back of my hand. "What's going on?"

I sigh. "The doctor is on her way in to talk to us."

As if I spoke her into existence, Doctor Diana walks into our room all smiles. "I heard you had a nap."

Sutton laughs, running her hand over her belly. "It was amazing. Still tired though."

"Rest is good." She steps over to the monitor, scanning the read-outs. "Last we checked, you were around eight centimeters?" Sutton nods her head. "Okay. Well, I don't want you to freak out, but the baby is showing some signs of distress."

My heart sinks to my stomach. We're in the hospital surrounded by medical professionals. This shouldn't be happening, but it is.

Sutton's hand squeezes mine. "What does that mean?"

"Labor is very intense for both you and the baby. You've been at this a long time, Sutton, and it's not getting any better. We can check you again to see if you're progressing to the pushing stage, but I need you to be open to a c-section. We're seeing baby's heart rate drop during contractions, which means they aren't getting enough oxygen."

Sutton's panicked eyes turn to me. I lean down and kiss her temple, stuck in the same loop of panic and anxiety.

Doctor Diana rubs Sutton's shoulder. "We're going to do everything we can for you to give birth vaginally, but I need you to be prepared. It's going to be busy in here, but we'll take good care of you."

"Do whatever you need to do," Sutton says, determination in her voice. "As long as everyone stays healthy, I don't care how the baby is born."

I nod before kissing her lips. "Healthy is good."

It's a whirlwind of an hour. Sutton's almost to nine centimeters, but she's still not progressing as much as they would like. Nurses have her turning back on her side, and an oxygen mask on. I'm sure they're doing a multitude of things, but all I can focus on is the fact that we can hear the baby's heart and Sutton is still breathing.

Still Breathing.

Still Beating.

Still Breathing.

Still Beating.

Doctor Diana comes back to check over the vitals. She purses her lips before saying something to one of the nurses, who promptly leaves the room.

"Sutton, it's time. Baby is still showing signs of distress, and I'm not comfortable waiting. We're prepping the OR for a cesarean, okay?" She's using that doctor tone I've heard Grant use many times. On the surface, she oozes calm, slowly letting Sutton know what's going to happen, but underneath it all is that hint of anxiousness.

Sutton's wide eyes pan to me before back at the doctor. "Can you talk me through it, please?"

I take her hand, listening to everything Doctor Diana says. She's straightforward, and I'm thankful for that. It helps to calm some of my nerves, and I'm hoping Sutton's too.

A nurse unlocks Sutton's bed while another one hands me blue paper scrubs. Sutton's got a bonnet covering her hair. She looks back at me, her eyes wide with panic as the bed moves to the doorway.

"Wait, can we wait a second?" I ask no one in particular and step up to her side. "I love you," I say, kissing her lips. "I'm going to be right behind you. I won't let go of your hand. I promise." Tears gather in her eyes as she nods her head.

She pulls me to her once more, kissing me firmly before she's wheeled away. "I love you."

SUTTON'S LIPS PURSE as she exhales through her mouth. Doctors and nurses crowd behind the screen, blocking our view of the surgery. Sutton's body shakes from the force of their movements, wincing. "Are you okay?"

She sucks in a breath. "It's a lot of pressure, but that's all I feel."

"Baby's head is out," comes a shout from the doctor. In a matter of seconds, a tiny squeal erupts from behind the screen. Tears stream down both our faces, relief and joy filling my chest. "It's a girl!"

A girl.

We have a daughter.

"Dad, do you want to cut the cord?" Loud, angry cries from our daughter echo in the cold operating room.

"Go," Sutton says. "Go take care of her."

I kiss her on the forehead through the surgical mask, squeezing her hand. This is everything I missed when Tristan was born. Tears stream freely down my face as I look at my daughter. Chubby cheeks with tufts of dark hair. She's not clean yet. A scowl sets across her face as she cries. Nurses scrub her down before offering me surgical scissors. I cut through the thick cord, following them as they take her to the warmer.

Nurses check her heartbeat and lungs, wrapping her in a blanket and hat before handing her to me.

There's no greater feeling than holding your child in your arms. "Hi, sweetheart. Are you ready to meet your mom?"

She doesn't settle until I place her on her mother's chest. Sutton cups her little head, tears streaming down her face. Love. Such immeasurable love lies in her eyes. "Hey, there little one." Lips brush against her forehead and she turns towards her. "I love you so much."

I stare down at two of the people I love most in the world, basking in the happiness and relief.

They're safe.

Chapter Fifteen

Sutton

My whole body is sore and I'm exhausted, but it was worth it. I knew labor was going to be no joke, but I couldn't have pictured it like this. Which I'm kind of grateful for, because otherwise, I'm not sure I would've been as calm as I was going into this.

We've had our share of visitors since our little girl was born: Wells' parents, my parents, our friends. It was nice that so many people came to see us, but I'm thankful that we're all alone.

Wells holds our daughter on his bare chest, getting as much skin-to-skin as he can. Even in pain after just having a baby, I can appreciate the view. Sneakily, I snap a picture of this quiet moment already planning to make it my lock screen background.

Our girl is so beautiful. Dark silky hair, chubby cheeks, puckered lips, ten fingers, ten toes. She looks just like her daddy, which I have to roll my eyes at. I only spent all these months creating a perfect living space for her just to spite me by looking like Wells.

"How about Margot?" Wells says softly as he adjusts her blanket over them.

My brows furrow. "Like Robbie? The actress?"

Wells chuckles, cupping our daughter's head so it doesn't bounce. "I was thinking more Christmas Vacation."

"Wait. You want to name our daughter after a character in a Christmas movie?" I laugh, wincing as it pulls on my stitches.

He shrugs, his eyes sparkling with amusement. "Just throwing out some ideas here."

For months, we've been brainstorming different names for both a boy and a girl. Not once have we agreed. "I don't think she looks like a Margot."

Wells stands cradling our newborn. "Here," I gently scoot to make room for them. He gingerly sits next to me, wrapping our daughter tightly in her blanket. He pulls me in close, placing our daughter on a nursing pillow between us. I sigh, leaning into his solid warmth, breathing in the smell of his skin.

We sit gazing lovingly at the little person we made. Our very special girl that brought the two of us together.

Warm lips press to my temple. "Thank you for this gift. I never thought I'd be blessed enough to have this again. To love someone like I love you. To have a daughter to cherish."

My heart soars. I cup his cheek, loving the feel of his day's old scruff against my palm. "I love you, Wells Green." He pulls me close, resting his chin on the top of my head. "What do you think of Sara being her middle name?" Wells stiffens beneath me, but I push on. "You loved her. She's the mother of her brother. I think it'd be nice to honor her in this way. Is that weird? Is it too much? Sorry, it was just a thought." I pull back, but Wells tightens his arms around me.

"No, I think it's nice." His voice is rough.

I lean back, looking up into his eyes. "Are you sure?" He kisses me, washing away any doubt I have. "At least we have a middle name," I snort.

"It's a start," he agrees.

We sit like this, volleying names back and forth, both vetoing ones we don't like. We resorted to looking up baby names on the internet. None of them seem to fit our precious little girl.

"Why is this so hard?" I whine, my frustration getting the best of me. "How did you come up with Tristan?"

Wells sighs. "Sara picked it. Tristan was her top choice since she was a kid. She named him after her grandfather."

I nod. "You got anything good?"

"Not unless you think Eugine would be a good choice for our daughter. You already shot down Etta," he says with a laugh.

"It's not that I don't like Etta. I just don't think it's her name."

"I agree." He rubs my arm in comfort.

My crazy hormones are turning me into a mess. "Why can't we figure out her name? I want her to have a name." My face scrunches as I try to hold back tears.

"Okay," he says softly. "We'll figure it out."

"Can you just name her? I don't know if I can handle it."

"No. Not doing that."

Damn it. I knew he'd say that, but I don't like this pressure. I sigh. Family members' names flicker through my head and one finally sticks out. "Reese."

Wells is quiet for a moment. "Reese." He strokes a finger down her pink cheek, her mouth popping open. "Is your name Reese?"

I smile down at my daughter. "Reese Sara Green. What do you think?"

Wells kisses me. "Her name is Reese."

"CAR SEAT IS READY TO go. Your bag is in the truck. What am I missing?" Wells checks every space in the hospital room.

Reese is tucked against me, letting out loud swallows as she eats. I almost had a breakdown when I couldn't get her to latch. It was like I was already failing at being a mom and she was going to starve to death. Kelly and Wells had to talk me down off the cliff. I might have been a bit overdramatic, but thankfully, it's all worked out.

"Did you steal the diapers and stuff? Kelly said they look the other way at that sort of thing. But, you know, I'm not sure how much we should trust her. She can be sneaky like that."

Wells laughs. "Grant said the same thing. Drawers have been raided and stuffed into the diaper bag that's..." He looks around, "Right here."

I laugh at his goofy grin. He's so much lighter now. His paranoia no longer has its hold on him. Sure, he still constantly checks on Reese and has Grant on speed dial even though he's given the full green light to go home. I love that he's so protective of his family and my heart soars to know that I'm one of them.

Nurse Kendra wheels in a chair. "Ready to go home?"

It's been three days since my surgery. Doctor Diana has been vigilant about checking in on me and making sure I'm recovering before sending me home.

"Yep. Paperwork is signed, birth certificate filled out, and I'm ready to crawl into bed and sleep."

Kendra laughs, locking the wheels. "Not sure how much of that you'll get."

I scoff. "Don't rain on my parade, Kendra. Let me live in my delusions a bit."

Wells laughs, pulling out a burp rag and handing it to me.

Reese's eyes are closed, her little mouth working, but she's done eating. I gently break the suction with a swipe of my finger, and she releases with a small pop. I set her in my lap and fix my clothing.

"May I?" Kendra asks, picking her up when I nod. She coos at my daughter, placing her on her shoulder to burp her. "You have a cutie, Momma. You did good."

"Thanks. She looks just like her dad."

"You're the only one that says that." Wells finishes packing up. I think he's more excited about getting home than I am.

"Just wait," Kendra assures me. "You're in there somewhere." She cradles Reese, cooing at her as she studies her features. "She really does look like her daddy."

"Thank you, Kendra. You've been the best nurse I could've asked for."

She nods, right as Reese burps. "It was my pleasure. Now let's get you home."

The ride home is quiet. After Reese gets strapped into her car seat, Wells and Kendra help me into the wheelchair. I'm not a fan of being pushed around, but walking hunched over through a hospital would've been worse. Wells drives slowly through town, apologizing each time the truck hits a bump.

Reese is perfect. I can't stop looking at her, running my finger down her cheek and over her eyebrows. She yawns, her mouth searching after my finger.

The truck rocks as we pull into the driveway and I hiss, my eyes squeezing shut while my sore body is jostled. This might be worse than labor.

Wells opens my door. "Home sweet home."

Tristan runs out of the house the second we walk up the driveway. "Where's my brother?"

With him getting sick so easily, Wells kept him at home. His parents have been watching him, taking him to school while Wells looks after us. Grant picked him up today and leans against the door, shaking his head and laughing.

Wells' shoulders shake with laughter as he carries our daughter inside, Tristan bouncing along after him. "I told you. You have a sister."

"A sister?" Tristan's face scrunches in disgust. He kneels in front of her car seat before glancing back at me. "How did she get out of your belly?"

I chuckle, lowering myself to the shitty couch. Wells is there in a heartbeat, placing a pillow behind my back. "Very carefully."

Grant chuckles, his keys jangling. "There's lasagna in the fridge. Hazel and her sister made it." He looks at Wells. "The directions are on the lid, so you can't mess it up."

Wells snorts, wrapping his friend in a quick hug. They exchange quiet words before Grant waves to me and walks out of the door.

Tristan talks softly to his sister. It's so precious that I watch them, tears pooling in my eyes. None of us expected life to turn out like this. Everything about it feels right. "You wanna hold her?" Tristan looks to his dad before nodding. "Come sit by me." I pat the space next to me and help him scramble onto the couch as Wells unbuckles Reese.

"You have to be gentle. Your sister is very little." Tristan's green eyes are wide as Wells slowly places Reese in his lap, supporting her head. "There you go."

Wells' face is the picture of happiness. Those green eyes are full of love as he looks down on his children, his smile wide. Tear rimmed eyes turn my way. Everything he isn't saying is there. All the sorrow, pain, worry, have been released, replaced by joy and love. Such love.

What started out as one night has turned into something more beautiful than I could've imagined.

Epilogue

Wells

A Year and a Half Later

"She should be here any minute."

Tristan peeks through the front windows to the street beyond. Grant's driveway across the street is loaded with cars to keep ours empty. It would be no fun to ruin the surprise, especially after all our planning.

I'm still amazed I was able to get the house ready in time. Sutton thought I was finally getting around to the changes we wanted to make when we first bought the house. It'd been a surprise. Reese was four months old when the house across the street from Grant went on the market. Four bedrooms, two bathrooms, and way more room than the starter house we brought Reese home to.

Our living room is packed with friends and family waiting for Sutton to come home. A "Congratulations Graduate" banner drapes across the entryway, complete with streamers. Kelly insisted on balloons that happily bounce along the ceiling.

Sutton worked so hard to get her masters completed. She spent late nights bouncing a crying Reese while reading textbooks, and devoted weekends to completing coursework. She may have had to take one more semester than she wanted, but I'm so proud of her.

"Dad, she's here." All three boys have their heads in the window before darting into the living room, laughing as they search for a hiding spot. They're taking the whole surprise aspect pretty seriously.

The garage door whirrs open and everyone falls silent. Even Reese, who's in Kelly's arms, looks around the room, her wide hazel eyes looking from person to person.

Keys clack on the kitchen counter. "Wells, what's going on at Grant and Hazel's? Is everything okay?" She comes into view as beautiful as the day we met. A chorus of "surprise" fills the house, stopping her in her tracks.

Sutton's face is frozen in a state of shock. Her eyes are saucers, her mouth open and tilted in a smile. "What's going on?"

Tristan runs up to her. "It's a surprise party."

Sutton laughs, running a hand through his hair. "Well, I'm surprised."

I wrap her in a hug, kissing her temple. "We wanted to celebrate all of your hard work. Congratulations, baby."

With Reese in her arms, Sutton goes around the room, hugging and thanking everyone for coming. Eventually, we spill out into the backyard into the cool late summer evening.

Joanna, the favorite of all our kids, stands in the yard watching as the kids run around. Cole chases after the boys with a giggling Marie hanging on his back. None of us were surprised when they finally made their relationship public. I've never seen Cole happier than when he's with her.

Hazel stands next to Joanna, the two women laughing as she sips her ginger ale. They just announced their pregnancy, and we couldn't be more thrilled for them.

Reese is tucked against my chest, her little finger brushing against the scruff of my chin as she fights sleep. Her mother is all smiles, laughing and chatting with her parents and brother.

"Someone's ready for bed," Grant chuckles, sitting next to me. "I'm about ready for bed myself."

I laugh. "And here Sutton calls me the old man."

"I don't know how you did it." He shakes his head. "Hazel's morning sickness has barely kicked in. Not bad, but I still don't like it. I can't imagine it lasting the whole nine months."

"It's tough, but they're tougher."

He nods, his eyes locking on his pregnant wife. "There's no doubt about that."

Reese has gone still, her breath hot on my neck. I kick Grant's foot, getting his attention. "Is she out?"

Grant leans forward. "Yep. Knocked out."

I stand and make my way into the house. Paper plates fill the trash bags, half the chocolate cake is eaten, and kids' juice packets haphazardly sit on the table.

I kiss my daughter's forehead, setting her into her crib. I study the slant of her brows, the pout of her lips, the flush of her cheeks. Her brown hair is just long enough to curl at the ends and I hope it's just like her mothers.

"Hey, you." Sutton wraps her arms around my waist, and I pull her close. "Man, she's really out, huh?" She looks down at our daughter.

"Yeah. Marie kept her busy." Cole's daughter has taken it upon herself to teach Reese everything. Marie dotes on her. When she was smaller, we had to keep a close eye on her, otherwise she'd try to pick Reese up and carry her around. Scared the shit out of us the first time it happened. And we made sure it didn't happen again.

Sutton nods. "Makes sense." She turns in my arms with a sigh. "Thank you." Hands run over my shoulders, her fingers twirling the hair at the nape of my neck.

"You deserve it." For the first time since this morning, I kiss her. Sutton melts into me, taking our kiss deeper. Down the hall, the bathroom door closes and we slowly break apart, remembering that we have company.

Sutton sighs, slipping from my grasp. "If you keep kissing me like that, we'll have another Reese on our hands."

I laugh. "I don't mind practicing." I've barely recovered from her pregnancy with Reese. Not that I don't want more kids, but I'm not ready for that right now.

She snorts, smacking my chest. My gaze settles on her retreating curves. I love every piece of this woman. From her determination and stubbornness to her never-ending patience and her loving heart.

Sutton pauses, hand outstretched for the knob. She turns a skeptical eye on me. "Is this why you've been more broody than normal? Too busy keeping a secret?"

I hold up my hands in innocence. "I don't brood. And I thought we discussed you analyzing me."

She moves back to me, and I can't stop myself from gripping her hips.

"It's hard not to wonder why the man I love is suddenly doing all the chores around the house. You tend to do busy work, you know." She places her hands on my chest, kissing me once more.

It's hard to imagine what life would be like without her in it. She transformed my world from shades of gray into vivid color, rekindling what I had lost, and giving me more than I could've imagined. "I love you."

Her smile is dazzling. "I love you, too."

Thanks For Reading

I hope you enjoyed Desired by the Single Dad!

A couple years ago when I came up with *The Single Dads Club*—the characters, the storylines—Wells was the only one I wasn't sure about. I knew he had a tragic backstory, but I wasn't sure how to move him forward. Then suddenly it hit!

Surprise pregnancy.

Setting up the timeline of events was an interesting one. *Desired by the Single Dad* starts at the beginning of *Nanny for the Single Dad* with the two plots crossing over at the park for Marie's birthday party. Planting the seeds about what the heck was going on with Wells was a lot of fun for me, especially since I was basically working on the two books simultaneously.

My favorite parts of this book to write, though, were Kelly and Sutton. The two of them together crack me up, so I hope they made you laugh, too.

Be on the lookout for more Briar Springs stories in the future! I'm not done with this town, that's for sure.

If you could, please take a moment to rate and review on Amazon, Goodreads, Instagram, or wherever you post reviews. As an indie author, ratings and reviews are the best way of getting my work out there for other people to read. A little goes a long way!

Don't forget to follow me on Instagram @authorsierrashipley and sign up for my newsletter to get freebies and see more details about my coming books!

Until next time,

SIERRA SHIPLEY

Sierra

About the Author

Sierra Shipley is a born and raised Midwest girl. She spends her days with her lovable rescue pup, Trip, who constantly wants all the cuddles, and her lovable cat Aidas. Her ideal day is spent drinking coffee, reading, and dreaming.

Sierra has always wanted the romance she's read in books. Pair that with an active imagination and a love of creativity, and you get a writer!

Sierra wants to create steamy, romantic stories with characters that people can relate to.

www.ingramcontent.com/pod-product-compliance
Lightning Source LLC
Chambersburg PA
CBHW030351180626
46812CB00007B/2840